DRAGON THIEF SERIES

SEASON ONE
Dragon Thief
The Chicago Job
The Poisons Book Job
The Vault Job
The Femme Fatale Job
The Scavenger Job

SEASON TWO
The Crown of Kingship Job
The Green Scroll Job
The Payback Job

THE SCAVENGER JOB
A DRAGON THIEF STORY

DRAGON THIEF
BOOK SIX

KAT SIMONS

T&D
PUBLISHING

THE SCAVENGER JOB

For my own hero, always.
And for my heroes in training...
Because they are doing so good at it so far!

ONE

Myra clung to Christopher's shoulders, her arms wrapped tightly around his neck as they soared over the city, his wings spread out above them, the nighttime New York City skyline below. The last day had been strange and complicated. And she was still deciding how she felt about it all.

Not that the last couple of months hadn't all been complicated and strange. Breaking into the dragon king's hoard had thrown her into a world she had never planned on visiting, nonetheless staying. And yet now, here she was. Happy to be in Christopher's arms. Happy they'd survived the last few days.

But leery of the world she now seemed to be

part of because she wanted to stay in Christopher's arms.

The night air bit sharply at her cheeks. Winter in full swing now. But the cold felt good. And Christopher's body temperature was so warm, she was comfortable in his arms during the flight.

A flight that had been her idea. They'd been dancing around their feelings for each other for the last few months. Or rather, she'd been dancing. In and out. Not sure if she really wanted to let more happen between them because it would mean staying at the edge of the dragon shifter world. Also not prepared to stop seeing him. Since they'd first met, she'd been attracted to him. Now, what she felt was…more. Enough she was willing to try something she never did.

They banked over Midtown, angling toward the west side of the island and his apartment at the top of one of the many high-rises in the area. Not the tallest building, but tall enough that his large open patio on the top floor gave him plenty of room to fly in and land. No need for elevators when you could do a partial shift and have wings.

As his feet settled onto the stone balcony, he tightened his grip on her, as if he didn't want to set her down. She didn't mind. She wasn't in a hurry to get out of his arms either.

"You're sure about this?" he asked.

Myra nodded. "Never been more sure of anything."

And after the last day, she meant those words with her whole being.

THE WATERS OF THE UPPER BAY FLOWED PAST AS Myra leaned over the edge of the ferry rail, enjoying the cut of the cold air and the whip of wind. When she looked up, the grand lady herself, the Statue of Liberty, stood glimmering in the sunlight across the water. Despite living in New York her entire life, she'd never been out to the statue. Maybe one day.

Now, she had other plans.

Which started in, of all places, Staten Island.

She loved riding on the Staten Island ferry, but she rarely got off and went into Staten Island. She hung out in St. George station, maybe got an ice cream, and then got back onto the next ferry returning to Manhattan. Mostly, she did this for the free boat ride. She could afford other options, she supposed. But when she was a kid, this free trip was what they could afford, and it had been one of her favorite things to do with her parents.

Still one of her favorite things to do.

"You're going to fall into the water." A deep

voice behind her. "And if you do, I'm not rescuing you."

She could hear both his worry and his hesitance. "Of course you will." She chuckled. "You couldn't resist rescuing me if you tried."

She smiled as she turned to face him. At nearly seven foot tall, Christopher's head came perilously close to the top of the roof on this lower deck. He sort of hunched to accommodate the occasional crossbeam, but it didn't help hide his size.

Nothing could really hide him when he was out among humans. Even without pictures of him out in public, she'd heard the others on the ferry whispering that he must be one of the dragon shifters. Which, he was. But fortunately, no one realized he was one of the dragon king's sons. There were no pictures of the royal family allowed in public. She hadn't understood why when the king had first informed her of the dictate. Now, after spending more time with Christopher, she realized it was a blessing for his sons, to have some semblance of privacy in a world that was *intensely* curious about them.

He really wasn't the kind of man who blended into the background, though. Dark messy hair, deep blue eyes, wide shoulders. There was a lot of potential for classical handsomeness to him, and yet he wasn't. The angles of his face were too sharp and the assembly of those features could have been described as awkward. No, not classically handsome. But compelling. Hard not to notice. Impossible not to look at twice.

She liked to think of his face as interesting. She was certainly interested in that face. Interested in the rest of him, too. And that interest had moved past simple lust now. Way past. Which was one of the many reasons for this trip to Staten Island. Even if he didn't realize it yet.

"I will absolutely let you fall into the river if you keep leaning so far over the rail," he said, hands on his hips.

She laughed. "First of all, we both know you wouldn't." He had a thing about damsels in distress. Couldn't let them remain in distress. Had to help. Some of the other dragons considered it a character flaw. She loved it about him. "Secondly, I can swim."

"Why am I not surprised."

"You're not? Damn, I'm becoming predictable."

"Never." His expression softened into a smile that made her stomach dance. She loved that smile. "Are you going to tell me what we're doing now?"

"Nope. It's a surprise."

"I'm not crazy about surprises."

"I know. But you'll love this one. I promise."

"Are we stealing anything?"

"Nothing that will be missed."

"That doesn't instill much confidence."

She winked. "You want some hot chocolate? It's a ferry tradition for me in the winter."

She was bundled up in a long wool coat, gloves, scarf, and thick wooly cap. Beneath she wore her work clothes. Black yoga pants, black shirt, her trusty, multi-pocket vest. But the coat, scarf, and hat were all bright. White coat. Red hat and scarf. Green gloves. She was a beacon of winter colors.

The expression on Christopher's face when they'd met at the ferry station, and she'd shown up wearing something that wasn't black, had been a delight to witness. The shock. And then the slow sweep of his gaze that had set those now familiar tingles dancing in her stomach. She had her hair down—which was rare—and had gone to the effort of wearing makeup. She even had mid-height, chunky-heeled boots on. The heels did nothing to get her anywhere near his height. He still had at least a foot and a half on her. But the heels made her calves look good in her tight leggings.

It was fun surprising him. She managed it occasionally. And she enjoyed it every time.

He was dressed for show, too. She appreciated that he'd even worn shoes so he didn't stand out too much. He hated wearing shoes for too long. His black wool winter coat and a scarf he sort of threw around his neck gave a nod to the winter. He needed neither. He could control his body temperature—most of the time—and didn't feel the cold the way a human might. When you flew and spent a lot of time at altitude with nothing but a few scales between you and the biting air, you needed to be able to stay warm.

He looked her over as another icy breeze blew across the open side of the bottom deck. There were only a few hearty souls out here. Most remained in the relative protection of the inside cabins.

"Hot chocolate would be good if it means getting you off that railing."

"I am not *on* the railing," she said, bumping her shoulder against his arm as she led him back inside. "If I were *on* the railing, I'd be closer to your height."

And she was not trying to draw that kind of attention on this trip.

With only a couple of days left till Christmas,

there were a lot more tourists on the ferry than usual for a winter afternoon on a weekend. If there was no compelling reason to take the ferry in the winter—like going to and from work—a lot of locals gave it a pass. But the ferry was, nonetheless, packed with people. Crowds inside making the lines at the snack stands surprisingly long. There were a few decorations up around the stand, some red and green tinsel, a menorah in honor of Hanukah, some fairy lights winking in white around the order window.

Myra loved this time of year. She liked the cold. But she also loved all the lights and twinkling colors. Not unlike actual treasure. Which she also loved.

The hot chocolate was delicious, though so hot she burned her tongue with her first sip.

"Can't take the heat?" Christopher asked, with a sexy smile.

"I can take heat just fine," she said, trying not to fall into his gaze and failing miserably.

"Need any help with the burn?" His gaze dropped to her mouth. "I could kiss it better."

Yeah he could.

A little purple light played over his irises, and his pupils were narrowed from the bright sunlight spilling in through all the windows lining the cabin. They'd taken a seat near a window that looked out toward the bridges. She loved the view of Lady Liberty, but watching the Brooklyn, Manhattan, and in the distance, the Williamsburg bridges was pretty stunning too. Definitely in New York with that view. But in that moment, all of her attention was captured by Christopher. And that faint purple light in his eyes.

Her stomach tumbled with now-familiar giddiness. Very soon they were going to have to do something about all this tension between them. And for her, very soon was sooner now than it had been a few months ago.

"We'd better wait on that kissing," she murmured. She was a little afraid if they started, she'd embarrass herself by forgetting they were in public.

That "forgetting herself" part had become increasingly more likely. And her resistance to forgetting herself increasingly thinner as the weeks rolled past. Everything about Christopher hit her lusty buttons and left her swoony. From his inability to resist a damsel in distress to his impressive height to the way he accepted her just as she was without trying to force her into a more conventional box.

Things with his father might be easier if she were a more ordinary human. Her being a thief, and a magical one at that, meant she was useful to the dragon king, but not his first choice for his son's romantic interests. Christopher didn't seem to care. And his father seemed to have given up any thought of interfering. At least, he'd made a show of giving up. Whether he had or not was anyone's guess. It was impossible to tell with the dragon king.

But the king had stopped attempting to hire her. Finally. Stopped trying to make her one of "his" people. Stopped trying to control her.

And that had made all the difference.

Now she just needed to do this one thing. One thing before "forgetting herself" completely.

Two

The house was a few blocks off the subway, which made getting there easy from the ferry station. But Christopher's impressive baring made the journey a little more obvious than it might have been if she'd gone on her own. Even sitting down, people couldn't stop staring at him. No one knew he was the king's son, but most ordinary humans deferred to dragon shifters if they recognized them. Something about the ability to breath fire inspired deference.

Christopher had been offered a seat the minute he stepped onto the subway. Which he'd proceeded to give up the moment a pregnant woman pushed a stroller into the carriage. And when the train reached her stop, Christopher and

Myra got off the train so he could help the woman get her stroller up the stairs. Which meant they'd had to wait for another train.

None of which Myra minded. The stairs were icy—it had snowed two days earlier, melted just enough to get everything wet, and then the temperature had dropped so everything froze over. The stairs would have been perilous for the pregnant woman. Myra was delighted Christopher even thought to help.

And, being completely honest with herself, his inability to *not* help was a complete turn on for her.

The snow started falling again as they waited on the open platform.

"We shouldn't have gotten off," Christopher said, hovering over her as if he could shield her from the snow.

She grinned up at him, letting some cold flakes hit her cheeks. "I like the snow. You think we'll still have any by Christmas?"

"The way the weather's been going, more likely a frozen East River and gray slush on the sidewalks."

"Hey, but then we could ice skate half way to Staten Island."

"I could have flown us here." He held his coat up so it acted as a makeshift umbrella, protecting her from the snow. The way he used his coat reminded her of the way he sometimes folded his wings over the top of her.

"I like the ferry."

"And the train?"

"Yes."

He dropped his chin and gave her a look.

"I do! But also, if we hadn't been on the train, who would have helped the pregnant woman get her stroller up the stairs?"

He shrugged and looked across the tracks to the platform opposite. But she didn't miss the color reddening his cheeks.

She leaned into him, letting his natural body heat keep her warm and pretending she liked the protection of his coat covering her head when what she really wanted was just to get closer to him.

They managed to stay on the train until their own stop this time. The walk was cold, the wind as sharp as it was when she flew with Christopher, but she barely felt that chill with him standing so close to her. He even held her hand for part of the way, ostensibly to keep her gloved fingers warm.

The feel of his huge hand wrapped her hers did more than keep her fingers warm.

When they reached the house, Myra spent several long moments just looking up at the place.

KAT SIMONS

She hadn't been here in years. She should have. She should have at least dropped in once or twice in the last ten years. But sometimes it was easier to leave all the past in the past.

She had kept tabs, over the years, checking in from a distance. Enough to know this was still the house. But standing here on the sidewalk, looking up at the narrow, two-story building, the white siding in need of a paint, the little front porch decorated for Christmas with twinkle lights around the overhand and some red ribbons circling up the posts beside the short staircase up to the porch. There was even an inflated snowman in one corner of the porch, bouncing around in the cold wind.

Myra couldn't decide if the decorations, slim though they were, made her happy or sad, so she chose happy that they were still there, and released Christopher's hand to walk up to the door.

Christopher hung back, following, but remaining on the stone pathway at the base of the stairs rather than following her up. Snow dusted the two narrow patches of grass that bracketed that path, but Myra remembered summers here when those tiny squares of grass were bordered by flowers and seemed like a huge yard to her.

She hesitated with her fist raised to knock, a

14

beat of uncertainty, before she gave the door a solid whack. She kept her hands out of her pockets, at her sides, ensuring they were in full view.

A few moments passed. She heard Christopher move behind her, remaining back but a tellingly restless movement. The door remained solidly closed, though Myra knew someone was at the peephole. She wondered if this was all she'd get after ten years. If this was her answer.

But then the door creaked open. Harry Goldsmidt stepped out.

Myra remembered thinking he was a huge man when she was a little girl. Towering and strong and indominable. A rock. He still had that craggy rock look to him, though older now, his pale skin creased in more places, his hair and trimmed mustache gray instead of brown. His glasses were thicker now, too, though still inside thin-rimmed frames. The thick cigar hanging out of his mouth was unlit. He was dressed in plaid pajama pants and a thick Irish wool sweater. The years had been kind. He wasn't hunched or too thin. He still looked sturdy and healthy—despite the cigar.

He just wasn't as huge as Myra had made him in her mind. Only a few inches taller than her. Shoulders she'd once thought broad enough to carry the world were narrower than in her memory. Looking at him through adult eyes without the nostalgia of kid memories to color what she saw, Harry looked like a perfectly ordinary older man. Glaring at her from his porch like he was about to shake his fist and tell her to get off his lawn.

That image made her smile. "Hey, Harry," she said. No matter what happened now, she was glad to see him, to see he was doing well. Glad she'd made this trip after so long.

A few moments of him scowling and staring at her. A moment when she worried she shouldn't have come back after all these years. Then his smile broke out huge around his cigar, and she found herself pulled into a bear hug. The familiar smell of his Old English deodorant and cigar smoke sank into her like coming home. A home she hadn't been to in a while.

"Myra, girl," Harry said, patting her back. "It's been a long time. Too long." He pulled back to take her shoulders in his hands and stare her in the face. Then he gave a brief nod. "You look like you've been doing okay for yourself. That's good. That's good. Your old dad would have been pleased."

"That's why I've come to talk to you, Harry. Though, I am sorry I stayed away so long." She gave a little shrug and had to look at the snowman on the porch when she said, "Memories are hard sometimes, you know."

"I know. I know." He glanced past her. "You've brought a friend."

"Harry, Christopher. Christpher, Harry."

"Nice to meet you," Christopher said, and there wasn't even a hint of curiosity or suspicion in his tone.

Myra found that very impressive given how curious and/or suspicious he must be at this stage.

"Yeah." Harry raised a shaggy gray brow at her. "A dragon, huh?" he murmured. "That'll take some telling. Though I'll leave it to you if you want to."

Harry had been as close as brothers with her father. The only real family they'd had beyond each other. An uncle, a confidant, the one they all knew they could rely on. And still there'd been secrets. Still there'd been a lot her father never told Harry. Things Myra had never told Harry even though she knew he was the one person she could trust. Harry understood that. Understood the secrets.

It was the reason her father had trusted him with everything.

She didn't respond to his curiosity about Christopher because that wasn't why she was here. "Can we come in for a few minutes or are you busy?" She'd been afraid if she called instead of just showed up, either he or she would have found an excuse to delay this reunion.

He nodded toward the house and stepped back inside, holding the door for them. Christopher ducked a little when he stepped inside. The door was barely tall enough for him to fit, but the ducking had to be habit at this stage.

The house was a little different than she remembered because ten years would do that to a place. The hardwood floors in most of the house were covered in a deep blue carpet now. That carpet had been a paler gray color the last time she'd been here. And where there was exposed hardwood in the entryway, that was covered with colorfully patterned Turkish rugs. Where there'd been a wood table in the narrow entryway with a bowl for keys and mail, there was now a series of hooks for coats, a larger hook for keys, and a smaller round table for the mail.

He'd once had a long mirror hanging near the door. There'd been a safe behind that mirror. The mirror was gone now and the wall smooth and painted. If the safe was still back there, it was even more cleverly disguised now.

A narrow staircase across from the door led up to the second floor. Past it, a narrow hallway that led back to the kitchen, which used to take up the whole back half of the house. There was a living room to the right. And a utility closet to the left. Upstairs, there were two bedrooms and a bathroom. Above that, a finished attic.

Narrow and simple. All he said he ever needed. Yard easy to take care of. Not a lot of maintenance. Easier to heat in the winter. All the excuses he used with her father when her dad had come into enough money to get Harry a bigger house.

A part of Myra was glad Harry never moved. This house had been the only consistent home she'd ever known.

"I've been nursing a pot of coffee all morning," Harry said. "You want to sit in the kitchen or the living room. I could start a fire. Got gas a few years ago." He grinned. "Get a fire whenever the mood strikes now."

His gaze danced to Christopher, a very large, hulking presence in the narrow hallway. Probably thinking Christopher could make a fire anytime he wanted too, but didn't need gas.

"Whatever's most comfortable for you," Myra said. "I need to talk about my dad, so…maybe the kitchen."

Harry narrowed his eyes a little behind his glasses, the low light in the hallway catching glints on the lenses and making it hard for her to read that narrow look.

"This way." He led them down the narrow hall to the kitchen, and Myra swore Christopher had to suck in his shoulders to get past the staircase.

The kitchen had changed since the last time she'd been here, too. Harry had upgraded his appliances to shiny chrome. The counter was still a light blue Formica, but the gas stove was newer. He also had a very fancy coffee machine on the counter that hadn't been there before. An open space, with a square wooden dining table against one wall, the fridge and stove against another, and a back door that led down two steps into the backyard.

Myra remembered thinking Harry must be rich to have such a grand backyard. She'd been four at the time, so everything seemed big. But that was before her dad had bought them one of the houses they'd lived in, when they'd still been living in an apartment and she'd thought only rich people had yards.

Harry gestured to the table, and one of the four high-backed wooden chairs around it. "Make yourselves comfortable. Do you want some coffee? I'll brew a new pot. I love this thing. The coffee is perfect. I make coffee all day in this thing."

"When did you get it?"

"Present from a lady friend for Hanukah last year. I still can't get enough of it."

Myra smiled. "And the lady friend?"

"Still around. Visiting one of her kids and his family upstate this week." He puttered around the kitchen, getting the complicated-looking machine going on a new pot of coffee. "Your timing was bad if you wanted to meet her, good if you wanted a private chat."

He glanced at Christopher, who hadn't spoken beyond the introductions, but didn't comment. "You take anything in your coffee now that you're an adult?"

She grinned. "Still like it milky and sweet, thanks."

"You?" Harry asked Christopher. "Or would you prefer tea?"

"I don't want to put you out," Christopher said. "Coffee is fine. Splash of milk is good."

Harry raised a brow. "If you're sure. With my new machine, boiling water is a snap."

Christopher's mouth twitched at one side, like a smile fighting to get out. "Tea then. Thank you."

Harry hummed as he worked at the coffee machine, seemingly delighted to give it multiple tasks at once.

Myra grinned at Christopher and he smiled

softly back, but she saw all the many questions in his eyes.

Harry brought over a small white ceramic pot with white and brown sugar cubes in it.

Myra raised her brows. "Fancy," she teased.

"Earned it after all these years," he said with a wink.

By the time they had their coffees and tea and everyone was settled at the table, some of Myra's nervous energy and worry had settled. But she still had a little flutter in her stomach as she met Harry's gaze and announced her reason for the visit.

"I need my dad's stash, Harry. I'm ready for it now."

THREE

Harry leaned back in his chair, the wood creaking faintly as he considered Myra over his steaming mug of coffee. The mug was a larger one with a picture of Florida on the side, something kitschy and touristy. Myra tried to hold his gaze as he studied her, tried not to blink. But it was hard after ten years. Especially when she was here for something she'd ignored for all that time.

"You sure, buttercup?" he asked.

The use of her old nickname nearly had tears welling. She forced them down. "I'm sure. It's time. I'm ready."

"Okay, then." He set his mug aside, placed his palms on the table, and levered up. "You two wait here. I'll be right back."

They waited quietly in the kitchen, each sipping on their tea. She heard the attic stairs come down, heard Harry walking around two floors up. When he'd been gone for a full five minutes, Christopher finally asked a question. "Why am I here?"

It wasn't the question she'd expected him to ask. She'd assumed he go right for the "what's happening" or "who is this" or any of the other many questions he no doubt had. The fact that his first wasn't to questions what she was doing, by why *he* was included was something she found… interesting.

"There's something I want to show you. It's important."

"Important," he said softly. Then nodded. And went back to drinking his tea.

Harry came down a few minutes later carrying a large wooden box. An ordinary one, not a fancy one. Something her mother had made in the early days, when she was new to woodworking and hadn't integrated it into her art yet. Just an ordinary square, dark wood box, with ordinary silver hinges and a ridiculous slip lock like you might find on a diary. Not even really a lock. Just a latch to hold the lid down and keep the contents inside from falling out.

"Here you go, buttercup," Harry said. He'd

managed to pick up another cigar from somewhere, still unlit, hanging out of his mouth again as he set the box on the table in front of her. "Your dad wasn't sure you'd ever want this. Considered tossing it away. I wouldn't let him."

She smiled, ran a hand over the worn wood, smooth but dusty, the edges of the lid a little wonky. "Thanks for keeping it."

"Does this mean I'll be seeing more of you around finally?" He sat down across from her again, set his unlit cigar next to the one he'd left on the table earlier, and picked up his coffee mug.

"You sure you want to? New life. Nice woman. No thieves coming and going to complicate things."

"You are who you are. Your dad was who he was. I take people for who they are. We're family. And ten years was too long."

She nodded, tightening her jaw to hold in the hot wash of emotions—guilt, love, regret, a little anger. "It was," she said. She flicked a look to Christopher, then back to Harry. "Still have a lot going on in my life that you might...prefer stayed well out of yours."

Harry's gaze jumped to Christopher, too. "Oh, I don't know. Been missing a little excitement in my life. So's Geraldine. Can't wait for the two of you to meet. Suspect you'll really like her."

Myra chuckled and dipped her head, her hand smoothing over the box lid again. "I need to go, to take care of this. But I won't stay gone this time. Maybe after Geraldine gets back, we can...visit."

"She'd like that. I've been telling her about you."

"You have?"

"Of course."

"And she still wants to met me?" Myra tried to joke but she was feeling a little choked up and the joke didn't land well.

Still, Harry took it for what it was. "Like I said, I think you two will get along well."

Something about the look in Harry's eyes, that twinkle that reminded her of back in the day, with Myra's dad... "I suspect you're right," she said.

She stood and took her coffee mug and Christopher's tea mug to the sink, only realizing she'd fallen into the habit half way to the open kitchen. When she returned to the table, she caught Harry smiling into his mug.

"Thanks again for this." She picked up the box. It wasn't heavy. Sturdy though. Not an aged cardboard about to fall apart. Her mom had used good wood. Wood her dad had somehow "found" for her.

Harry walked them to the door and Myra hesitated on the step, reluctant to leave, even though this was something she needed to do. The snow had stopped again, leaving barely a dusting on the ground under the sidewalk trees.

"I'll be in touch after the holidays," she said, attempting to memorize Harry's face as he was now. Not the man in her memory, but the living, breathing Harry Goldsmidt of today, with his unlit cigar tucked between his teeth on one side of his mouth, his thick-lensed glasses. His soft sweater and plaid pajama bottoms. The additional lines on his face. The gray in his hair and mustache. "It's good seeing you again, Harry."

"You too," he said. "Good luck with that." He nodded to the box. "Hope we get a chance to talk about it after."

On the walk back to the train, Christopher held his questions. Once they'd gone down the stairs and were waiting on the platform heading back to St. George station and the ferry, he stopped waiting. There were no other people on the platform. The traffic on the road above was light. The open valley that made up the station and tracks left little cover if it started snowing again. But since it wasn't, Myra walked them to the end of the platform so they could be on the back of the train.

"Where now?" he asked. Moving to stand in a way that blocked her from the wind.

She hid her smile, but she did wonder if he even realized he was doing that. It didn't look like he was aware of making the adjustment. "Now we get somewhere quiet and I open the box."

"This is what you wanted to show me? The important thing."

She nodded.

"Something inside the box. What it is?"

"Ah, that's the trick. It's not so much what's inside, but where it leads."

His brows snapped down over his eyes, which looked particularly blue in the winter's gray-white lighting. "Where does it lead?"

She grinned outright this time, because she was talking to a dragon shifter. "Treasure."

FOUR

Myra picked up their tail about two minutes slower than she normally would have, and she kicked herself for that oversight. She had been lost in thought—about Christopher, her parents, Harry—and thinking about the box on her lap. She had only peripherally noticed the man who joined them on the platform. Habit meant she'd taken in his bearing—middle height, thick with muscles, dark hair, pale skin made red in the cold. He was dressed in jeans, jacket, boots. Nothing really stood out about him except for maybe the tattoo on his neck poking up above his collar, but otherwise, just a man on the train platform.

She should have guessed something was up, though, when he moved back through the doors

29

between train cars to join them in their mostly empty rear carriage. Did, as it happened, realize something was up. Just about two minutes slower than she should have.

Leaning into Christopher, like she was snuggling with him, she reached up and gave him a kiss on the cheek, then whispered, "Dark haired guy with the gray puffy coat."

"Spotted him."

Of course he had. And that only made her more irritated with herself for realizing so late.

"Any idea why?" Christopher whispered in her ear, making it look like he was nuzzling her neck.

Myra had to work not to get distracted by the nuzzle, though. The feel of his breath on her skin sent a shocking spear of desire shooting through her. Shocking because he wasn't even trying.

She smiled and hummed and tried to look like she was so into her companion she wasn't aware of anyone else on the train—barely a leap given how the feel of Christopher's light kiss on her ear sent sensation zinging through her.

She turned into him so their mouths were a breath apart and said, "The box." Her hand tightened on it convulsively.

"Someone wants whatever is where that box is leading?" Christopher murmured before setting his lips to hers.

The kiss, soft and gentle and obviously part of a play to fool their tail, nevertheless robbed her of thought for a full forty seconds. She just wanted to sink into his kiss, sink into his heat, and it took her brain too long to remember she couldn't yet.

Then, "All I can think of. Unless someone else is tailing us for an unknown reason." She couldn't think of any immediate person who might want them followed. Except maybe... "Your father?"

"That's not a dragon," Christopher said, dragging his lips along her jaw, to the sensitive spot just under her ear.

Wow, was concentrating tough when they did this. She blinked up at the subway ceiling, pale, lined with air vents currently not on. Metal hand olds bending over the row of seats against the wall...

"Your father would know you'd pick up a dragon following you. Would he send a human?"

Christopher growled. The sound did nothing to ease the heat coursing through her. In fact, it ratcheted up the melting sensation.

"He might," Christopher admitted. "But why follow us out here?"

"He's nosy?" And he didn't approve of their relationship. And maybe he was just worried she'd lead his son into trouble.

Which...might happen. But honestly, she'd

been in more trouble lately because of the king himself. And Christopher was well able to get himself into trouble all on his own thanks to his soft spot for damsels in distress. Neither of them needed *her* to stir up danger.

"I could always ask," Christopher said against her ear.

She shivered. She just couldn't help it. "We could," she said. "Or we could see what he does." She was curious enough to let the tail follow them for a bit just to see what he attempted. But she didn't want him following to her father's "treasure." That was one of the reasons this box had remained in Harry's attic all these years.

The train pulled into the next station. The man stayed seated while two teenage girls with very big hair got off, three men in construction gear got on, and another man who seemed to be alone got on, his face in his phone.

The face in the phone was actually a pretty good way to appear harmless. Myra had used it herself more than once. It didn't work this time. But mostly because she was on guard now that she'd spotted the other tail.

"Two now," she murmured, smiling up at Christopher and batting her eyelashes.

She watched his mouth twitch like he wanted

to smile, or laugh at her lashes move, but then a crease formed between his brows in a frown.

"We should get off," he said. "See what they do."

"Yup. Also put fewer people in danger if they aren't just keeping tabs on us for your father." And with two of them on the carriage now, she doubted this was just a find-and-report for the dragon king. This was something else.

The three construction workers and the remaining older woman with her dog tucked into a large bag could be in danger if things went sideways. Neither Myra nor Christopher wanted that. And Christopher could get hurt trying to protect innocent bystanders.

They continued to pretend to be completely absorbed with each other—not much of a stretch, really not that much of a stretch for her—and waited until the train slowed and pulled into the next station. They weren't that far from the last stop, but the ferry station would have a *lot* more innocent bystanders around.

Christopher stood and helped her to her feet as the train bounced to a stop. Then they sauntered off as if they were in no hurry and had nowhere in particular to go, Christopher with his arm slung around her, keeping her tight to his side, her with her parents' box tightly clenched in her arms.

The man with his face in his phone got off while still making a show of reading his phone. The gray puffer jacket man rushed off just as the doors were about to close, like he'd forgotten this was his stop. The two men walked ahead of her and Christopher, not looking back at them as they all slowly moved toward the stairs at the other end of the platform.

Letting all the other people who'd gotten off get safely away from whatever happened next.

There were a handful of people across the track on the other platform, but the train going in the opposite direction pulled in just then, giving them more cover.

"I could always just fly us away," Christopher said as they watched the two men in front of them.

"Then we wouldn't know who sent them and why they're following us," she pointed out. Though she was tempted.

If the dragon king had sent them, it would amuse her to slip the tail. If it was something to do with her parents' box, she didn't want them continuing to tail her and Christopher.

But knowing which of the two options applied —or if there was some third, so far unknown, option—was a bit of information she didn't want to let go.

Her job, her life, hinged on information.

Leaving without knowing who these guys were and why they were following her and Christopher might put her and Christopher in danger later.

Once the opposite train pulled out of the station, Myra looked around. No one had gotten off, and the few people who'd been there had gotten on the train. The two platforms were currently empty. Except for the two men, and her and Christopher.

Almost as if they'd all decided they were in the clear to talk now, the two men turned, simultaneously, to face them.

Myra smiled. "Good afternoon, boys. What can we do for you?"

The man with the phone tucked his phone into his pants' pocket as he simultaneously pulled out a gun from his coat pocket. "You can give us that box."

FIVE

Well, Myra had her answer. The two men following her and Christopher wanted her father's secrets. She only realized she'd kind of been hoping this was just the dragon king being a pain in the ass when she saw the phone-guy's gun. She wasn't crazy about guns. Definitely didn't like having them pointed at her. Or at Christopher.

Especially at Christopher. Because he'd tried to save her from a bullet. He wouldn't ever be able to help himself.

The air on the open platform was cold against her skin, but Christopher was like having a furnace at her side, he pumped off so much heat. The sky overhead was gray, but no new snow fell. She wasn't sure if that was good or not. Would snow help or hurt their chances of getting out of this without that gun going off?

The second man in the gray puffer jacket also pulled out a gun. And Myra sighed. Two guns definitely made this more complicated.

"The box is a Christmas present from my dad," she said, scanning their surroundings casually, looking for options. "I'm afraid I'll have to say no to your polite request to take the box. Anything else we can do for you?"

"You could die," the man in the puffer jacket said. His voice was gravely and low. And something about it was vaguely familiar though he, himself didn't look familiar to her.

"No thank you," she said with a grin. "I'm having too much fun to shuffle off this mortal coil just yet."

Christopher, true to his nature, stepped just a little in front of her at the threat from puffer jacket, and the hissing growl he issued was that distinctly dragon shifter sound that no human vocal cords could make. The sound always made the hair on her neck rise, but also did a little melty, tingly thing to her insides because he usually made that sound to warn off people threating her.

He was so sweet.

"Your father stole something from us," the man who'd been on his phone on the train said.

His dark hair barely fluttered as a cold wind blew down the tunnel of the train platform, a sign of some very impressive hair product. "We want it back."

"It won't be this." Myra patted the box. "Whatever he stole, he stole it years ago and probably sold it off a month after he took it. I'd suggest looking elsewhere."

"We know exactly what's in that box," Phone-Guy said.

"That's impressive, since I don't." Which was, technically, true. She didn't know precisely what was in the box. That was really the point. But if she didn't, she was certain they didn't. Even Harry might not know exactly what her father had tucked away into that box, and Harry had had the thing in his attic for ten years.

"Your father was a fucking thief," Puffer Jacket said.

Myra shrugged, nodded, and frowned all at once. "Yes. Yes, he was. I thought that was already well established." She nearly made a Captain Obvious joke, but thought better of it, what with all the guns.

Puffer Jacket opened his mouth again but snapped it shut at a raised hand from Phone-Guy. "We don't have time for this. Hand over the box or we'll shoot you."

KAT SIMONS

Christopher issued that growling hiss again. And really, the two men with the guns should have been more aware of the danger they were in. But she had no idea what happened if Christopher got shot. Whether it was deadly for him or some shifter trick would let him survive. She wasn't sure if bullets would even have any impact on him.

In dragon form, traditional bullets were less than useless. They just bounced off dragon scales like cotton balls. That was one of the main reasons world governments had negotiated truces and treaties with dragon shifters when they'd come out of their caves and into the open. Who the hell wants to tangle with something that breaths fire and can't be shot down? Everyone made good faith deals, and humans and dragons had been living relatively peacefully side-by-side ever since.

The other shifters had come out after, and at different times. The magic wielders interspersed throughout that same period. And the world had gotten very interesting in the fifty years since. She'd always known a world with shifters and magic wielders existed. But Harry had told her stories of a time before, when the magical part of her father's skills had to be kept quiet.

Puffer Jacket flashed Christopher a teeth-

40

heavy grin. "Wanna try something there, big boy? You think you can take us when we got two guns. I don't see any scales."

"He breaths fire, you know," Myra said matter-of-factly, but with a little confusion. Antagonizing a dragon shifter when you realized they were a dragon shifter was just…what? Suicidal? Yeah, suicidal seemed the best description. "Are you trying to get killed? Is that the thing here? Suicide by dragon? That's a bad idea."

"Shut up," Phone-Guy said.

She couldn't tell if he was talking to her or his accomplice, so she just grinned and kept talking. "Listen, you guys aren't getting this box. Whatever my dad stole from you—and I'm not denying he did, by the way. He was a very good thief—but whatever it was, it's well gone. My dad didn't keep loot. He sold it. And used the money to buy things and do things. None of it was left when he died. So this box isn't going to help you."

"He wouldn't have been able to sell this," Phone-Guy said. "And our boss wants it back."

"A mysterious boss now? Groovy. But I'm telling you, he didn't keep anything."

Which was true as far as it went. This box did lead to his treasure. But his treasure wasn't all the things he'd stolen for money.

And there was a difference between the things he'd stolen for money and the other things he'd stolen. She just couldn't imagine these guys would be ten years' worth of committed to anything her dad had stolen for non-money reasons.

"He kept this," Phone-Guy said, sounding very sure of himself. "And we've been trying to find it for ten years. We want it back. His daughter is gonna get it for us."

"Or what?"

"Or we'll turn you over to the cops."

She actually laughed. "For what?"

She committed lots of thefts, of course. There were any number of things that could get her sent to jail if there was actually evidence of the break-ins. But she didn't leave behind evidence of break-ins.

"We'll come up with something," Phone-Guy assured. "Notorious daughter of a notorious thief has a lot of skeletons in the closet, right. And everyone knows it was you who broke into the dragon king's hoard. Cops won't have trouble believing anything we feed them."

The dragon king's hoard thing was really going to follow her around. Probably good no one knew about the female dragon's hoard but the dragons.

"Good luck," she said.

"You ain't worried?"

"Why should I be? I'll either go to jail, or I won't." She shrugged. "And you still won't have found whatever it is you're looking for because my dad didn't have it. Though, maybe, if you tell me what it is you've been looking for, I can find it for you. Get it back. For a price."

Christopher didn't glance back at her, or growl, or comment. But she noticed his shoulders stiffen and wondered if he thought she was being serious.

"We'll just take the box. And maybe we won't kill you."

"As I said, even if you took the box, it'll be no good to you. You won't understand the contents." She might not know *exactly* what was inside, but she knew her father, and she knew it wouldn't be obvious to anyone what it was.

Phone-Guy waved his gun at her. "Set the box down and walk backward. I'm done talking."

"So are we," Christopher said.

And the hairs on Myra's neck stood up. His voice was deep, gravely, and the hiss was more obvious.

He took one step forward, putting a foot of distance between her and him. She nearly closed that distance, afraid he was going to try taking a bullet for her.

But in the next instant, his coat shimmered, a swirl of purple fog whipped around him. And she thought he was going full dragon. A move that was...probably bad on the narrow train platform.

She heard the click of guns. Heard Christopher's growling hiss. And then his wings snapped out behind him.

Myra had half a beat to realize he'd done the partial shift without even removing his shirt and coat. And then she was in his arms and they were heading toward the sky.

Behind her, she heard gunfire, but it sounded very far away.

SIX

"Well," Myra said once her heart dropped from her throat back to her chest after the rapid ascent. "That was unexpected."

Christopher's wings beat the air three times before he even glanced down at her. At this height, the wind was brutally cold, biting at her cheeks and making tears leak from her eyes. She leaned farther into his warmth. Except he wasn't just warm. He was hot. Like leaning into a furnace. Which meant there were a lot of emotions happening just then.

He was shirtless now, too, with just the layer of purple and yellow scales across his shoulders and upper chest. But given the amount of heat he was pumping out, she knew he wasn't cold.

She clutched her parents' box to her stomach with both arms because Christopher hadn't even given her enough time to get one arm around his neck. Not that she needed that. He cradled her with one arm beneath her knees and one around her back and she felt perfectly secure and safe.

The amount of trust she had in this man still stunned her. That she knew in the depths of her soul he wouldn't drop her.

They were far above the train station now, well out of range for the guns the two thugs had had. She was a little sorry they hadn't revealed what they were after, but she couldn't be upset with Christopher for getting them out of there.

"Are you cloaking now?" she asked.

He grunted once, still not looking directly at her. That was a little worrying. But the cloaking at least meant the men couldn't follow. To them, she and Christopher disappeared into the air. And there was no telling where they'd end up.

They were safe. So why was he avoiding her gaze?

"You gonna tell me what's wrong while we're up here or after we land?" she asked, louder than she might have on the ground, but the wind was noisy up here.

"Nothing's wrong. Where are we going now?"

He sounded strange. And something most

definitely was wrong. But obviously they'd have to deal with that when they landed.

"Anywhere we land is fine for the moment," she said. "I need to open the box, so somewhere with relative privacy would be good." She scanned the island below, looking for a convenient rooftop. There weren't the number of skyscrapers and high-rises here in Staten Island. But there were enough tall buildings to give them a few choices for landing. "Head west. See that building." She pointed. "Top of that should do."

Christopher banked and headed toward the multi-story brick building without a word.

When they landed, he folded his wings against his back, but didn't reverse the partial shift that had produced his wings. He set her on her feet gently. He was always gentle. But his jaw was tight, and his mouth a hard line.

He did not look like a happy man.

"Okay," she said with a sigh. "Before I open this, spill. What's with the angry face?"

"Two men just tried to shoot you. That tends to spark my anger."

"Not the first time." Though, to be fair, when they'd first met and a wizard had hit her with magic and almost killed her, Christopher had fried the wizard and the shifters working with him. And that was before they'd gotten close. So she

47

supposed endangering her did spark his anger. Still. "Is this about me pretending to offer to find whatever it was they were looking for?"

"Of course not," he snapped, and she raised her brows at him. He let out a breath and, in a less sharp voice, said, "I know you don't work for other people. Besides, I could smell the truth."

"Okay. Then what has you all bent out of shape."

"Besides the two men trying to kill you?"

"Yes."

He let out a snort that might have been a laugh if he hadn't been so upset. Then said, "Your father put you into danger."

She dropped her chin and looked at him. "I put me into danger. And your father puts you into danger. All the time. Your father puts *me* into danger. What's your point?"

"Those men..." He sucked in air through his teeth and glanced away. "They stank of resentment. And the one in the gray coat had... unpleasant things on his mind."

"Murder or other unpleasant things?" She could guess. The type of people her dad had sometimes gotten mixed up with were not opposed to some truly horrendous acts, with murder only the tip of the horrendous iceberg. That was one of the reasons Myra didn't work for other people. She never wanted to deal with the kinds of associates her father had sometimes dealt with.

"Other unpleasant things," Christopher said with a snarl.

She nodded. Made sense why he was so upset now. "I'm a little surprised you didn't crisp them."

"Close thing."

She smiled. With obvious reluctance, his shoulders relaxed and he let out an almost smile. Not quite ready to let go of what had just happened, but willing to move on.

Or so she thought. "What if they try to find you again?" he asked. "Or do go to the police with some trumped up charges?"

"They go to the police, we'll deal with that. I'm pretty good at staying out of jail." Not out of trouble. She got into trouble all the time. But she was good at staying out of jail. "And I doubt they'll find me again. They only found me this time because they've probably been staking out Harry's place."

"For ten years?"

"I know right? I have no idea what they think my father took from their boss, but this was a long time to wait to get it back."

"Why didn't they break into Harry's to get the box?"

"Good question. No idea really. But maybe their boss knew what's in here won't mean anything to anyone but me."

"You said you didn't know what was in there."

"I don't. Not specifically. But I know what it's supposed to be. And it wouldn't do them any good." In fact, she wouldn't be surprised if they had, at some point in the last ten years, broken into Harry's place for the box. And then realized it didn't help them without her.

But that would mean they probably did know specifically what was inside when she didn't, and that was annoying as hell.

"So now what?" Christopher asked, more of the tension in his shoulders relaxing.

He still had his wings out. But as a cold breeze blew across the rooftop, she had to wonder if he wasn't a little cold without a shirt on.

"I didn't know you could partial shift with your clothes on." She gestured at his bare chest. "Will the clothes come back when you tuck your wings away?"

He gave a short nod.

"Handy. Aren't you cold?"

"Do I feel cold?" He wrapped one big hand around her waist and eased her close.

She moved the box to her hip so she could

better lean into him and his heat. "No," she said quietly. "You don't feel cold at all."

He leaned down as she went up on her toes, meeting in the middle for a kiss that reignited the edgy, needy tingles that had burned through her on the train when they'd supposedly been pretending at the PDA. She couldn't have Christopher's lips on her, his breath fanning her face, his heat and scent surrounding her, and not react.

A not insignificant part of her wanted to abandon this mission of hers. It wasn't absolutely necessary. She could go home with him, take him to bed, lose herself in him without this. She could be close to him, be with him, without him having to know this.

Couldn't she?

As his mouth angled over hers, his tongue sweeping into her mouth, dancing with hers, his arms holding her tight, his scent filling her head, she almost abandoned her mission. Came within a breath of telling him to just take her back to his place and they'd forget the box.

But then, if she did that, if she didn't follow through with this, she knew she'd regret it.

This legacy first. This revelation.

And then… Well, then she had ever intention of getting Christopher out of his pants.

She eased out of the kiss, but didn't drop back

to her feet, keeping her face close to his, letting his shallow breaths brush over her cheeks. Her heart was pounding harder than when they'd leapt into the air, and she could feel his heart thumping under her palm where she had her one free hand pressed to his chest.

He cleared his throat, swallowed visibly, before saying, "We need to finish whatever this is we're doing."

She raised her brows.

"With the box. With your father's…present? Legacy?"

"Both," she said. "And yes, we do."

"Okay. Then what do we do now?"

She dropped back from him, smiling when he released his hold on her only reluctantly, and then she sat down abruptly on the roof. The move so sudden, in fact, Christopher reached for her as if he thought she was falling. She grinned up at him, a long way up, the gray clouds at his back making a halo around him with the dim sunlight filtering through. She crossed her legs and settled the box into her lap.

"Now," she said, "we open this present from my dad and see what he left me."

SEVEN

Myra waited patiently for Christopher to settle next to her on the flat rooftop. As she waited, she took in the surroundings. A pretty ordinary rooftop—she'd been on many, enough to know the ordinary ones from the extraordinary ones, like the ones with hidden pigeon coops and really fancy water towers. This one had the usual fans and extraction ducts, glistening coldly in the gray winter light. The roof was treated with a black, weather resistance tar that was a little sticky under her. The door into the building was around the opposite side of a small raised shed to her left.

Below, traffic skuttled past. And if she turned just right, she could see the island of Manhattan and the Statue of Liberty. Probably if she stared long enough in that direction, she'd see the Staden Island ferry chugging through the bay.

The snow that was thickening in the gray clouds overhead continued to stay away. But the wind was icy. Sitting on the roof helped protect her from that wind a little. The heat pumping off Christopher warmed her even more. He was like one of those standing heat units that restaurants set up in their outdoor seating areas so they could leave those open in the winter.

He stared down at her for a long moment, his wings puffing a little behind him. She did enjoy him shirtless, but the wind fluttering the thin membranes of his sturdy wings still looked cold to her despite all that heat coming from him. The purple and yellow scales across his shoulders and chest were easier to see but more muted in the winter light. They shimmered when he moved though.

And then they flowed away when he did that partial shift that retracked his wings completely. A swirl of purple, sparkly fog wound around his upper body briefly. When it faded, he stood in his fully human form, no more wings, no more scales, and his shirt and coat back in place.

"That swirly fog stuff is the magic that enables the clothing thing, isn't it?" she asked, shading her eyes with one had so she could keep looking at him while he hovered over her.

He finally sat beside her. Dropping into a cross-legged seat with a surprising ease and grace for a man that big. "Yes." His voice was gruff.

"So, when you don't need to worry about your clothes, you can snap out your wings and put them away without all the swirling fog. But when you need to get rid of clothes or when you take your full dragon form, then swirling fog. Right?"

"Right."

"Groovy."

She'd only seen his full dragon that one time, when they were escaping a very angry female dragon. And it had been a very impressive dragon form at that. But up until then, he had only every snapped out his wings around her, and then, only when he was shirtless. He was starting to show her more and more of his shifter nature.

That was nice. Especially since she was about to show him more of her nature. Something he needed to see and understand. At least, she *wanted* him to see and understand.

She didn't know where this thing with them was going—besides eventually to bed—but she knew, for her at least, it was getting a lot more serious than a simple fling. Or even a friends-with-benefits thing.

They were, and had always been, more than friends. The fact that she could call him a friend, too, only proved how much more serious this was for her.

And if she was going to get serious with a man like Christopher, he needed to see her as she was. The parts of her she'd shown him, he accepted. Even if some of her love of jumping off the side of buildings gave him heart attacks. Now it was time to show him a part of her that really only Harry and her parents knew about.

She swallowed and patted the box. "It doesn't look like much, I know. And you won't understand what's inside. I'm asking you to trust me. To trust me to show you…what all this means."

He held her gaze, and to her pleasure, didn't nod immediately. He took a moment to think, to consider what she'd just said. So that when he nodded, and said, "I trust you," she could believe him because she'd watched him come to that conclusion right in front of her.

"Okay. Here we go." She flicked the latch holding the lid down with her thumb and opened it, its plain metal hinges stiff from disuse. Once she had the lid up, it stayed raised on those old hinges, making it easier for her to study the contents of the box.

She smiled. "Thanks, dad."

Inside was a small wooden sphere, made from multicolored pieces of different wood—one strip oak, another bamboo, a third pine—all interlocked and wrapped around each other. The sphere wasn't smooth like a ball, but multifaceted, almost like a Christmas tree ornament. In fact, if she hadn't known what it really was, it could look like nothing more than a handmade ornament. That's probably even what the thugs and their boss thought it was at first. Maybe that's why it had taken them ten years to come for her and the box. Maybe they'd assumed for a long time this was all it was, a nothing. And they'd only recently learned it was more than a decoration.

"What is it?" Christopher asked, leaning forward to look at the sphere inside the box.

"It's a puzzle." Myra grinned up at him. "I love puzzles. And this one—" she looked back down into the box again, "—requires magic to figure it out."

And not just any magic. Thief magic. The kind of magic she and her father shared.

She let her fingers hover over the sphere, just above a narrow strip of oak, and smiled at the tickling feel of the magic. She could sense the spells, the power. Sense the threads of the puzzle.

It was a very nice sensation. It reminded her of her dad.

She studied the sphere both visibly and with her magic, found the places to push, to slide, to move the different little pieces of wood. The sphere looked like it would open at one point, then another piece had to be moved and it covered up the hole. More pieces slid. A click. The feel of one part of the magic snapping open.

A lock and a puzzle all clicking and dropping into place. With each move of the physical puzzle, she had to make a simultaneous move of the magical puzzle. Slowly finessing the locks that held the pieces in place in order to move them.

A particularly clever magical lock rose up at a crucial place in the physical puzzle and made her chuckle. "That one was tricky," she murmured. Her eyes were half closed as she focused on the game her father had left her. Her vision taken up by the sphere's wooden pieces and the magic she could see in her mind's eye as well as feel.

Each twist, each movement, each unclicked lock, brought the puzzle slowly, slowly to opening, to revealing what her dad had hidden.

Peripherally, she was aware of the cold air blowing across her cheeks, of the presence of Christopher, still radiating an enormous amount of heat, of the distant traffic and the sounds of seagulls screeching out over the bay. But most of her was inside the puzzle.

And when the last magical lock opened under her nudge and push, when she slid the last physical piece of the wooden sphere into the right place, she let out a triumphant laugh. As the sphere opened wide in her palm.

The clever wooden ball turned into a sort of open flower, the wooden pieces flaring like a rose, each "petal" spreading wide to reveal a hollow center. Inside was a small key, the sort of key that might open a kid's diary, just a tiny bit of tin. Next to the key a piece of paper folded small enough to fit.

She looked up at Christopher, smiling. "Brilliant, isn't it?"

Christopher had creases along his forehead and his brows were bunched. He just looked confused. "Those are the treasures? A key and a piece of paper?"

"Those are the next clues," she said. "What fun would this be if it was easy?"

"Clue? As in… Your father left you a scavenger hunt?"

"Yes." She beamed. "He told me before… Well, before he and my mother were killed, he said he intended on leaving me a scavenger hunt as his last act. That he thought I'd enjoy that better than hearing some stuffy lawyer read out what I was left with. He knew me well."

This made Christopher's scowl soften into almost a smile, but the smile couldn't hold out against his confusion.

"When he… When we talked about that," she went on, "about him dying, I figured that would be fifty years later, when he died of old age while breaking into some impossible-to-crack vault somewhere." She chuckled at the remembered image she'd had of her dad, in his nineties, breaking into a vault successfully, then laying down and dying peacefully on the floor.

She got more serious when she said, "I didn't expect to lose them so soon after that conversation. I've wondered, over the last ten years, if my dad didn't suspect something. Have some sort of premonition. If my mom maybe had some sort of flashing insight that she'd told him. I don't know. Neither of them were psychic. But the accident happened maybe six, seven months after we had that conversation about a puzzle-filled scavenger hunt. And it was more than a week after their death before I found out he'd set up the hunt. I just sort of assumed, since their deaths were sudden, that he wouldn't have gotten around to it yet."

"Why didn't you do the hunt before?"

She stood abruptly, and Christopher, looking

startled, flowed up with her. He hunted the area as if looking for a threat.

"I don't want to lose the light," she said. "We should get going." She pocketed the little key and tucked the now open puzzle sphere back into the box. The little piece of paper, she opened and read. And smiled. "Very clever, dad," she murmured.

"What?"

"A riddle. But it's got a glimmer of magic over it, so what's on the page isn't the real riddle." She showed Christopher the note.

He frowned and read, "Twelve gulls and a pint of beer for Janice." His scowl deepened. "What the hell does that mean?"

"Nothing." She chuckled. "Like I said. It's a cover. You need thief magic to decipher it."

"So what's it really say?"

She appreciated that he didn't return to the question she'd not so elegantly avoided. She'd tell him why she'd been avoiding this scavenger hunt once they reached the end of it. That was half the point of bringing him along. To…explain things to him. But she wasn't ready for that part of the conversation yet. Not until she'd followed the clues to the end of her dad's game.

"What it really says is that we need to go back

to Manhattan, to a building downtown not too far from the ferry station."

He narrowed his eyes. "You got all that in a few words?"

"I solved my dad's riddle. The riddle won't make sense to you." She shrugged at his frown and said, "The actual riddle is, 'Where Howard lost his shoe that one time.' And unless you know that Howard was a friend of my father's before he met my mom, and had heard the story about how my dad and Howard had tried to rob a bodega once and gotten chased out by the bodega cat, you would have no idea what that meant."

Christopher's lips twitched. "Got chased out by a bodega cat?"

"They are the best of cats, friendly to all who enter. Unless you're entering when you're not supposed to and you accidentally step on their tail."

His lip twitch turned into a grin. "Fair enough. Not much of a riddle for you, though."

"I never said my dad was good at riddles, just good at hiding things. The trick will be finding what he hid at the bodega where Howard lost his shoe that one time."

Christopher looked out over the bay. "Those men will probably be waiting for us at the ferry station. Or even on the other side in Manhattan."

"Maybe." She sighed. She loved flying with Christopher, but she'd sort of wanted to do this scavenger hunt as her dad had intended, and taken that excuse to ride the ferry back. But needs must. "Do you mind flying us back?"

"Of course not. I adore flying with you."

The expression in his eyes made her heart pound harder, reminding her why she was doing all this now. She dropped her gaze to the box, assuring everything was safely back in place and the box was latched shut. When she got home, she wanted to reassemble the sphere and set it to do what it had been originally designed to do.

Christopher lifted her chin with the side of his finger, forcing her gaze up to his. He searched her expression for a long moment and it took a lot of effort on her part not to try dropping her gaze again. Being that vulnerable, that open… That was what all this was about for her, and yet it was still incredibly difficult. She was used to hiding almost everything about her real self from everyone she knew. She didn't want to do that with Christopher. But old habits die hard.

After an intense moment, he released his hold on her chin and gave a little nod, as if he'd just decided something. Then he stepped away from her a few feet and the swirling fog circled him again, briefly. When he stepped out of the sparkling purple mist, he was shirtless again, his wings spreading out wide behind him.

She cradled the box in her arms as he stalked toward her and gasped when he swept her up and took flight in one motion. The thrill as they climbed high made her laugh. She looked up in time to catch him grinning down at her.

Even without all this, the man did know her pretty well.

Eight

Her father's clue was near the back of the bodega, and the fact that it was still in place was a testament to the sturdiness of the resident bodega cat and the consistency of the bodega itself. The cat in question was not the same one who'd chased Howard and her father out of the store, of course. Sturdy or not, that had been forty years ago and no cat that wasn't a shifter lived that long. But one of that cat's offspring had remained in residence and was just as protective of their home as their mother had been.

The bodega itself was a typical one of its kind. This particular place long and a little narrow. The shelves along one wall filled with chocolate and chips and protein bars. The opposite wall lined with glass door refrigerators filled with drinks. There was enough room at the back for two central shelves, which contained mostly food staples like cereal and pasta and soup, and one self was lined with non-edible things like paper towels and toiletries.

There was a small selection of random items like pain killers and replacement earbuds at the front next to a counter where fresh sandwiches and baked goods kept the office dwellers in fast lunches and breakfasts. This particular shop even had shelf where customers could pour themselves out a cup of ordinary coffee—no fancy flavored lattes and cappuccinos here—and tart it up with milk and sugar as they liked. When the pots were full, this place probably smelled strongly of coffee, but whether because of the waning afternoon or the proprietor's indifference, the pots were now empty.

This late in the afternoon, in the last days before Christmas, with most of the businesses in the surrounding office buildings closing for the holiday, the bodega was mostly empty but for a few people who'd come in on the last ferry and the cashier, who was sitting behind the register desk flipping through a magazine as he spoke loudly into his cellphone.

The bodega cat in residence was sleeping on

an ancient cat bed near the back of the store, pushed up onto one of the shelves near cans of dog food which looked older than Myra. With Christopher acting as lookout, she knelt on the sticky floor and gently nudged the cat and its bed to one side. The cat opened its eyes briefly, gave her a teeth-revealing yawn, then proceeded to stare at her as she hunted the back of the shelf behind the bed.

It took her almost a full minute to locate the broken, wobbly piece in the shelf's wood, and to get it pulled out, all with the cat remaining stubbornly in the way. The fact that it wasn't attacking her or yowling and drawing attention was a minor miracle, so Myra was inclined not to do more than she was already doing to nudge the cat to one side. After some stretching and finagling, she removed the tiny box that had been shoved inside the secret hidey hole, and replaced the loose piece of wood to cover the hole again on the off chance that someone actually got brave enough to remove the bodega cat's bed and search back there.

She thought that was unlikely, though, given the sheer size of this cat. Not quite as big as a Maine coon, but big enough, its gray and black fur fluffy and soft. She grinned at the cat when she settled its bed back into place, gave it a scritch around its ears and head. This started it purring.

When she stood, Christopher, who was still mostly watching the front of the store to make sure they weren't disturbed, gave her a look.

She shrugged. "Payment for letting me move him around."

"Good show for the camera, too." Christopher nodded to the close circuit camera up near the ceiling, pointed at the rear of the store to discourage shoplifters.

"True, if the camera were an issue. But it's pointed far enough to the left, I wasn't being picked up."

"How did you know that?"

"Habit and a good eye for what security cameras are actually pointing at." She shrugged. "Part of the job."

She patted his chest—he was back to his shirt and coat because the wings, or even being shirtless, would have made them stand out too much as they came into the shop—then she grabbed a bottle of soda from one of the fridges and paid for it at the register. The cashier barely glanced at her, his full attention still on his phone call.

Out on the sidewalk, around the corner from the bodega, she pulled out the little box from her coat pocket, where she'd tucked it, and then handed Christopher her unopened soda bottle to hold along with the larger box he'd been carrying since they landed.

"Another box," he said.

"Another box."

A small, dark wood box with a lid that lifted completely off, the entire thing small enough to fit into the palm of her hand. She could have hidden it just by closing her fist. This one was actually locked, though, unlike the larger box Harry had been holding for her. A turning number lock, similar to the type of thing found on luggage locks, where she had to enter the right series of numbers to get it to open. There was a small spell on the lock, but it was just there to keep anyone from breaking the entire locking mechanism off. Opening the lock itself didn't require magic. Was simply a matter of entering the right code. Something anyone could do.

"Do you know the code?" Christopher asked, his gaze scanning their surroundings.

The downtown area was incredibly quiet, with a few cars passing on the main streets, but on the side street where they stood sheltered against the back of a building, there wasn't any traffic or pedestrians passing.

"That's the trick," she murmured, considering

the lock and what code it might be. Not her birthday. Or her mother's. That would be too obvious. Her father hadn't known his real birthday, so he'd just celebrated on January first every year. Probably not that either. She needed six numbers, so a date of some kind seemed likely.

After a few minutes of hovering behind Christopher as he blocked her from the wind and kept her warm with all his body heat, she grinned. Ah. That had to be it. She flicked the numbers into place.

The lock clicked open.

"What was it?" Christopher asked, looking down at her and the box.

"The date of the cat incident. The date Howard lost his shoe being chased out of the bodega by a cat."

"Huh. That should have been obvious. But I'm surprised your dad remembered the date so precisely. Precisely enough to tell you."

"Well, it was the first time he met my mother, so it was a date that made an impression."

"First time?"

"That particular meeting didn't go so well." She chuckled. "He had to find her again before she'd give him the time of day."

Christopher raised a brow. "Like mother like daughter?"

Her stomach did a fluttery dance even though she wasn't entirely sure why. She hadn't made him come looking for her after their first meeting.

She'd waited until their third meeting before she'd made him come look for her.

"What's inside?" he asked. He leaned in closer, his arm resting against the wall beside her head so he could get a better look at the box in her hand. The position was a little distracting, though, because she was surrounded by his heat and his scent—his ordinary scent of musk and dragon and an earthy leather undertone, not the scent of sugar cookies that he sometimes smelled like to her— and it made concentrating on the box difficult when all she really wanted to do was pull his mouth to hers.

Later, she promised herself. Later.

She sucked in a deep breath and lifted the lid off the box.

Inside was a tiny glass Christmas ornament. Very tiny. The size of her thumb, with a little bit of silver string at the top for hanging the tiny ball on a tree. It was a soft, almost muted red color, and there was a miniature picture on it. It was so delicate, she handed Christopher the little box it had been in so she could handle the ornament carefully, one hand holding it while the other hand cupped beneath it in case it dropped.

She held it up to the light to better see the image painted on the curved glass.

"A Christmas tree on a Christmas tree ornament?" Christopher asked.

"Not just any Christmas tree." She studied the pictures. There. A tiny ice rink. That narrowed the tree down to two obvious places. But which one… She leaned in closer to see all the tiny details. "Ah! There we go." She held it so Christopher could see better. "See the tiny sitting lion under the tree like a present?"

Christopher frowned as he nodded.

"The Bryant Park Christmas tree." She grinned. When he continued to frown, she said, "Okay, see the ice rink next to the tree? That's either Bryant Park or Rockefeller Center. The lion is from in front of the New York Public Library…"

"Which is next to Bryant Park," he said as the light dawned. "So we're heading to Bryant Park."

"We are."

"It will be mobbed."

True enough. The downtown areas and office buildings might be quiet two days before Christmas, but the holiday market and ice scatting rink in Bryant Park were going to be wall-to-wall people.

"We'll have to manage," she said. "Dad's next clue is there."

"But...the tree is temporary. There's hardly a clue on the tree."

"No. It'll just be somewhere in the park. We'll need to look at some of the permanent structures." And hope, all these years later, the next clue hadn't vanished.

She pushed worry about that aside. "Subway," she said. "I don't want to make a dramatic entrance into a crowded part of town."

"I could land us on a roof and we could come down the elevator like normal people."

"First, no one is ever fooled into thinking you're a normal person. Second, that sounds like a better plan." Mostly because now that she was on the scent, she wanted to get there fast. And dragon flight was significantly faster than the subway.

She looked around their surroundings. There were a few people passing on the crosswalk, but once the lights changed, things got quiet. Only a few cars moving past. "We'd better hurry before we attract an audience."

The purple fog swirled around Christopher again, and a moment later, he was shirtless with wings.

She shook her head as she gently placed the tiny ornament back into the tiny box he handed back to her, and put the whole thing into her pocket. "Gonna have to get used to knowing you can do this partial shift even with clothes on," she murmured.

"Does it bother you?"

She blinked. "No. Of course not. Just...I'd gotten used to you needing to be shirtless. Watching clothes appear and disappear is different. That's all. But I'll adapt. It's not like I haven't seen it before."

She'd seen another shifter go from full dragon, down to a man fully clothed and then back to dragon again before she'd even seen Christopher's dragon.

She took the larger box back from him, then set her free hand to his now bare chest and grinned. "I just like when you're shirtless."

That earned her a smile that made her toes curl.

In the next moment, she was in his arms. His wings beat downward twice and they were aloft, rising up over the skyscrapers in moments. Christopher circled once and then turned north. Heading toward Midtown and Bryant Park.

And hopefully their next clue.

NINE

They found the next box hidden in the statue of William Cullen Bryant. Well, more to the point, in the base of the statue. The domed marble portico held up by columns around the bronze statue glistened in the lights from the holiday market stalls. Down a row of stalls and rising majestically above them, the brightly lit Christmas tree dominated the part of the park closest to the library. Beyond the tree, the huge, seasonal ice rink was brightly lit and busy, the music loud enough Myra could hear it over all the other people and conversations.

The area behind the booths near the statue wasn't quite as crowded as the rest of the park, but there were a couple of booths bracketing the statue, so there were still quite a lot of people pressed tightly together, trying hard to squeeze into the booths and buy last minute artisan presents. The afternoon was waning now, the lights inside the glass-covered stalls starting to glow, the lights on the giant tree brightening. The area around the statue was dark, and protected enough from the wind to be less cold than out near the rink.

Myra had Christopher sit on the steps up to the statue to keep watch—sitting because he was less obviously huge and intimidating when he was sitting—while she hunted the area around the base of the statue.

She considered searching up higher, climbing to the top of the structure surrounding the statue, but decided her father would leave his clue somewhere that didn't make finding it too obvious. A woman scaling the statue's portico would be pretty obvious. Not that that wouldn't be fun to try and get away with. But she'd need to wait until it was dark. So she searched the base of the statue first.

"You're sure it will be with this statue?" Christopher asked quietly as she moved behind him.

"It's the best spot to ensure what he hid stayed

hidden for as long as necessary. Most of the other options are too exposed."

And the statue was one of the permanent fixtures in the park, here since 1911. Not likely to be moved or otherwise disturbed. Which made it ideal.

The little square cutout at the very back of the base of the statue was almost impossible to see. The lines blended in with the marble and looked like they were just joints that were part of the base's construction. Unless you were looking for it, the odd square shape just wouldn't jump out.

It took her several moments to figure out how to open the hatch, though. She pressed different sides of the square. She attempted to pry it out with one of her lock picks. She even tried a little open spell. None of it worked.

So that meant the opening latch was somewhere not on the square itself. She hunted for a button or a soft spot in the statue's base and finally found a little bump on the portico's floor, by one of the columns. Pressing it with her fingers, she realized it also needed a spell. That took another few seconds, figuring out which one triggered the locking mechanism. It turned out to be one of the more obscure spells her father had taught her when she was first learning about her magic.

That sparked a memory of sitting with him outside the apartment building they'd been living in at the time, on a low brick wall that held up a tiny patch of greenery and a single bush, and teaching her the words to this spell. She smiled at that memory, one she hadn't looked at in years.

Then she opened the secret hatch.

The square of marble popped open enough for her to get her fingers behind it and pry it out. She reached inside the little hole, pulled out a brass cylinder, and replaced the square so that the marble base looked smooth and undisturbed again.

Sitting on the step beside Christopher, she showed him the cylinder. About six inches long, decorated with a swirling pattern on the outside, topped at each end with decorative endcaps. All on its own, the cylinder was probably worth a tidy sum. It was, to Myra's trained eye, an antique, probably Egyptian, and infused with enough residual magic, she felt the tingling against her palm.

"Pretty," Christopher said. "Is it the clue or does it have something inside?"

"Haven't opened it yet so I don't know." She considered whether the scroll itself might be the clue because unlike the first box she'd gotten from Harry, which Christopher held in his lap, or the tiny box hidden in the bodega, which was tucked into her coat pocket, this was actually an objectively valuable piece. Probably part of the clue, at least. Her dad wouldn't have just tucked something like this away without a reason.

She considered the end caps, how to open the cylinder, spotted the little pressure point, and pressed it. One end cap clicked open, popping out on a hinge so suddenly, Myra thought the cap might go flying. She glanced around, making sure no one was watching—anyone who passed ignored her and Christopher—then she looked into the cylinder. Inside, she could just see a rolled-up piece of paper.

Easing the paper out, she realized it was papyrus. "Going the extra mile, huh, dad," she murmured, mostly to herself. The papyrus didn't have any words on it, not even hieroglyphs, which wouldn't have surprised her. There was just a picture of a blue hippopotamus with a flower on its side.

"Make any sense?" Christopher asked, studying the picture over her shoulder.

This one was trickier than the first message. At a glance, she could assume this led to the Met Museum because of the extensive Egyptian exhibit there. If that were the case, they were in a little trouble because without looking at a clock, she knew it was late enough that the Met was probably either closed or closing soon. Breaking into one of the major art museums in the world would be fun—she'd done it only once before— but it required time. And planning. And probably just waiting till morning and going in with all the other visitors would be easier.

But given that museum exhibits moved around a lot, sometimes went on tour to other museums, and sometimes were just tucked away in basements while other artifacts went on display, she wasn't sure her father would have chosen the Met. The little hippo and the papyrus definitely hinted that the cylinder itself was Egyptian. Where else might her dad mean for her to go besides the Met?

When her eyebrows popped up at the possibility, Christopher's gaze sharpened. "What? What's wrong?"

"Not...wrong, so much as, a little more complicated." She blinked at him. "One time, my dad was hired by a man who turned out to work for the Egyptian embassy. The job was to steal back an Egyptian artifact that had been illegally taken from the country but was in the hands of someone wealthy enough the diplomates, and even the US government, hadn't wanted to question him. It wasn't a big artifact. And there wasn't enough proof for the customs department to risk pissing this particular guy off." She shrugged. "I also think the Egyptian diplomat just didn't want to go through the hassle or paperwork and red tape that would have been required to get the artifact back and returned to Egypt. So he found and hired my dad to steal it."

"Your dad got it?"

"That. And a few more things he didn't mention to the diplomat. The extra stuff he sold and that's when we moved into our first actual house. The first of several we lived in. But that was one of his best scores, between the money the diplomat paid him and the other things he'd stolen. He'd gotten better at his craft at that point and got away with the heist. No one ever knew what happened to the artifact 'officially,' but my dad told me it made it safely back to Egypt and is in the basement of the Cairo Museum for safe keeping."

"A worthy theft."

"He thought so. He loved being able to give my mom a house, too." She rubbed a finger over the cylinder. "He and the diplomat became... friends of a sort. They worked together a few more times, successfully, and my dad was invited into the embassy a few times."

"You think the next clue is in the Egyptian embassy? That's going to be…difficult."

"Not the embassy itself. Too much risk of it being found in their regular security sweeps. But the diplomat had a nice apartment on the Upper East Side. That building had a mosaic of a hippopotamus on the lobby floor. Not a blue one, just an ordinary hippo in the middle of a jungle. You had to stand back and really look to even see it. The diplomat thought it was good luck."

"We won't be able to tear up a mosaic in a public lobby without drawing attention," Christopher pointed out.

"It won't be something that obvious. But the next clue is in that building."

"So to the Upper East Side, then." Christopher stood smoothly and held his hand out to her, still cradling the larger box in his other arm.

She took hold of his hand and let him lift her because there was something thrilling about that show of strength and she wasn't ashamed to admit it.

Rerolling the little papyrus page back up, she slipped it into the cylinder and stuck the whole thing in her coat pocket next to the tiny box from the bodega. She might need to get a bag to carry all these clues and treasures soon.

"Taxi, subway, or flight?" she asked. Flight

would mean going up to the roof of one of the surrounding buildings, but it would also get them uptown in minutes, so on balance, the time was about the same for their various options.

"Flight," Christopher said. "Fewer witnesses to see where we go."

She raised her brows. "Still worried about the thugs from Staten Island?"

"I doubt they've given up this easily."

True enough. But how they'd possibly follow them when she and Christopher were flying around this city, him cloaked from observers, she wasn't sure. But as they left the park to return to the building they'd landed on getting here, she heard a few whispers in their wake, whispers about Christopher, suspicion that he was one of the dragons.

He was not an inconspicuous man. Even if the thugs from Staten Island weren't able to follow them, too many people noticed Christopher. He just couldn't blend into his surroundings very well. People noticing you meant determined people could find you by asking the right questions. She had no idea who the thugs' boss was or if that boss had extensive connections of informants. But better safe than sorry. Keeping their movements as concealed as possible seemed smart.

She just hoped her dad's scavenger hunt didn't lead them to places were being concealed or lost in a crowd would be impossible.

That was already difficult enough with a dragon shifter companion.

TEN

They found the next clue in the mosaic itself. Nothing she could take with her. But some of the tiles had been replaced, a subtle change creating a subtle message. She wasn't sure how her father had even managed it. But the change, when looked at from the right angle and with a little bit of magic to see through the illusion spell, pointed the way to their next location.

"The armory?" Christopher asked as they traveled up in the elevator to the apartment building's top floor. Pretending they were here to see someone to get past the doorman might have been trickier if Christopher hadn't convinced him that his father—the dragon king—was interested in buying one of the apartments in the building, but the whole purchase and viewing process had to be kept secret.

The doorman had no problem believing Christopher was a dragon shifter. Believing he was one of the king's sons only took a few extra minutes of convincing. Since there were no photos of the royal princes anywhere, people didn't really know what Christopher or any of his brothers looked like. But it wasn't much of a stretch to see him as the son of the dragon king. People *did* know what the king looked like.

The armory was closed by the time they reached it, of course, but her father hadn't intended them to go inside. The armory was only about twenty blocks south of the hippo apartment building, so they reached it quickly. Christopher landed on the roof of the massive, block-sized, red brick structure, near the central tower of the administration building.

Myra smiled as she looked over the edge of the crenellated roof to the gray granite coat of arms in the center of the top level of the tower.

"You're sure your father would have hidden something there?" Christopher leaned over the parapet too, scowling.

"He would. He knew how much I liked scaling buildings."

She set a temporary spell on the armory

security camera on the roof, to keep it from recording all this, then handed Christopher her pretty white coat which had been great for blending in with humans but would get in the way here.

"I could hover in front of that coat of arms for you to find the clue," Christopher pointed out.

"Where would be the fun in that?"

She pulled a grappling hook from her multi-pocket vest and secured it between the brick parapets, the gap between crenellations narrow enough to make a secure hold for the hook. She secured the wire to her vest, winked at Christopher, and rolled over the side of the building, letting the wire catch her after a ten second free fall.

Christopher watched her every move as she scaled down the wall, her booted feet on the bricks, her gloved hands holding the repelling wire. She walked down until she was level with the coat of arms plaque, then hunted around the smooth gray granite until she found her father's next clue.

When she got back up to the roof, Christopher helped her over the edge. "What was it this time?"

She showed him the crystal bobble that had been imbedded inside one of the nooks in the carved coat of arms and then disguised with an illusion spell.

"A bell?" Christopher raised his brows at her.

"A very specific kind of bell," she said.

"And it means?"

"Saint Patrick's Cathedral."

HER DAD HAD LEFT HER A TOUR OF THE CITY. A tour of memories. From Howard's shoe, to the Egyptian diplomat, to the priest at St. Patrick's who'd caught her father trying to steal a candle when he was a teenager and proceeded to teach him about forgiveness. For years, until the priest was transferred to another parish, her father had come to visit him at St. Patrick's, and they had sat up in the northern tower near the bells to talk because her father had felt safest up high.

She'd inherited that from him. She felt safer the higher up she was. At the top of buildings, on roofs, the place she ended up a lot with Christopher…

There was probably a point to be made about that.

The next clue was tapped inside one of the nineteen bells and it required a little more maneuvering to get at. If she'd been alone, she'd have had to use a rope and lower herself to the appropriate bell from above, or used some of her magical suction grips to hold onto the outside of the bell while she pulled the piece of paper out.

But Christopher just reached across the giant gap of open space, grabbed the end of the bell, and pulled the eight-hundred-pound monster close to the circling catwalk so she could grab the note—fortunately her dad had left the note in one of the midsized bells. Myra wasn't sure even Christopher could have dragged one of the multi-thousand-pound bells close. And if he could have... She wasn't sure what she'd have done with that information. Except the thought gave her a little thrill of excitement.

He eased the bell back into place so it didn't make noise or draw attention. The bells weren't scheduled to go off again until morning, so one of them suddenly making noise would definitely be noticeable.

The note inside the bell, led them back downtown. This time to Battery Park and the SeaGlass Carousel. A place her father had taken her only once, but she'd been enchanted by the lights and music and the way the fish "swam" behind the glass. She'd enjoyed riding the carousel, but she'd enjoyed watching the fish almost as much as the ride. And she'd loved spending that evening with her father.

The next clue was a thin brass box, shaped like an envelope, with a flap sealed by a spinning lock that had to be opened using a specific letter code this time. It only took her a few minutes thought to solve this one. It was the first letters of her name, her mom's name, and her dad's name in order.

"M. A. P." She chuckled. "Dad used to find it very funny that our initials spelled map."

"Because it was like a treasure map?" Christopher asked.

"Exactly." Her heart did a funny little flip.

"I know Myra," he said. "A and P stand for?"

"Alana and Peter."

"You haven't said either of their names before this. Harry didn't say your father's name either when talking about him."

She shrugged. "Habit. None of us used names often because we never knew who might be listening." She frowned. "I didn't even realize I was doing that. Or that Harry hadn't mentioned dad's name."

"Names for dragons...mean things. They're important. We don't take them, or the use of them, lightly either."

"That's why none of you like having your names shortened?"

Christopher growled if someone tried to call him Chris. Myra had met other dragons who had the same reaction to the mention of shortening their names. She'd suspected names were important. And she knew dragons only gave each other their names under specific circumstances, a custom that meant they often forgot to introduce themselves by name. But *why* any of that was so wasn't in any of the public information she'd found researching dragon shifters.

"When we're given a name," Christopher said quietly, the lights from the carousel reflecting behind him and giving him a bluish halo, "that name holds...weight. Power, but not the way wizards don't like their real names to be known because it can be used in spells and things. Our names are... I'm not sure how to put this. Protective. Distinct. *Us* to other dragons. Like our scent is us. Altering or changing or shortening the names feels like it...diminishes us. On an instinctive level that we don't completely control."

"Ah. I had wondered. But I couldn't find the 'why' anywhere."

"We don't talk about it to outsiders," he said. "It isn't public information."

That funny flip in her chest, her heart

pounding harder again. Because he'd just implied she was not an outsider among the dragon shifters. That felt a little momentous.

Also a little terrifying.

But she enjoyed a little light terror.

Christopher's eyes glowed slightly purple in the dim park light as he held her gaze. Then he blinked and nodded to the brass envelope. "What's the next clue?"

She reached into the thin rectangle and pulled out a dog tag. The next code was written in braille.

"My dad's mom was blind and taught him braille," she told Christopher. "He taught me, but I'm rusty. It's been a few years." She closed her eyes and let her sensitive finger tips move over the raised, patterned bumps. When she finally read the message, she nodded. Of course. "We're off to Queens."

"Queens?"

"Queens."

ELEVEN

The cemetery had closed at sunset and had been closed for hours. It was well after midnight now, the scavenger hunt having taken them all around the city for the entire afternoon and half the night.

To finally end up here.

"You're sure this is the end of the hunt?" Christopher asked as he landed gentle in the middle of the grounds, carefully setting down on the road through the cemetery instead of on the grass and any of the graves.

Calvary Cemetery near Woodside in Queens was a wide-open patch of land with gentle hills, lots of open grassy space, and a few copses of trees. At night, the raised headstones and occasional monument loomed like watchers, waiting to see what she and Christopher would do. The wind was harsher here, colder, because of all the open space. The temperature had dropped steadily all evening. And now, out in the open like this, Myra felt the cold more than she had during the day. Even without snow.

Lights from the surrounding city, and the just visible glow of Manhattan, turned the cloud cover orange, adding a strange sort of light to the dark graveyard.

"I'm sure this is the end of the hunt," she said. "This is where my grandmother is buried."

"Your father led you to your grandmother's grave?"

"No. Well, not technically. I mean, he didn't bury his treasures in her grave, if that's what you're worried about. I don't have to dig up her coffin or anything."

"That's a relief."

"He was a thief and a conman, but not a grave robber. He knew I loved puzzles. He wouldn't have ended all this fun with something gross."

"So...we're not going to your grandmother's grave?"

"We might swing past before leaving. But why we're here is a tomb set in a small hill not far from her grave. When I was a kid, he'd bring me here with him to pay his respects to his mother. I didn't know her well, by the way, except for visiting her here. She died when I was about two so I don't have any real memories of her alive. But I thought of this place as 'visiting grandma,' and it was a nice day out in greenery with my dad and sometimes both mom and dad. But I was a kid. So I got bored and wandered off among the stones, enjoying having so much grass and so many trees around me."

"You weren't scared? It's a graveyard."

She shrugged. "Not a scary one in the middle of the day. Pretty. And like I said, lots of grass and trees and open space. Not a normal part of my day-to-day at that time."

She adjusted her coat with one hand as she led him along one of the smaller roads winding through the place. She'd taken the larger box back from him for the flight here and carried it cradled in one arm. It now also held the Egyptian cylinder, the brass envelope, and the smaller box she'd tucked into her pocket earlier in the hunt. She never had gotten a bag to carry everything, but she wanted to keep all the little notes and treasures together because they'd been left by her father. The box was heavier now than it had been, but she didn't mind.

"Anyway," she said, "I frequently went exploring while they attended the grave, and once,

I found this really nice tomb. It looked like a little house. I guess I was about seven or eight at the time, and I thought it was a house for people who'd died. I even knocked to see if I could come in."

"You wanted to visit the dead people?" He gave her an incredulous look.

"I was a kid. And we were already here visiting dead people. I thought actually seeing someone might be a nice change of pace."

The cold wind blew her hair across her face and she tucked it back behind her ears. She glanced up at the cloudy sky, lit orange from the city lights, and judged they had another half hour before more snow fell.

"The tomb's wooden door was locked of course," she continued. "There was no metal gate over it or anything. Just the wooden door and a key lock. It required one of those big keys. The old-fashioned kind. With the long neck and decorative head? Which, of course, I didn't have on me."

"But I suppose that didn't stop you."

She laughed. "It did not. I did have my new lockpicks on me—present for my last birthday—and I decided this was a great way to practice."

"You picked the lock and broke into a tomb." He shook his head, but there was a glint of humor in his eyes and that soft purple glow filled the blue now. "Grave robber child."

"I was just going to *visit* the dead people, not steal their stuff." She bumped up against his arm with her shoulder. He was too tall for her to bump his shoulder. In response, he took hold of her free hand, cradling it in his big grip as they wandered down the road. Even through her gloves she felt his warmth.

"So you broke into the tomb?"

"I broke into the tomb. And was very disappointed not to see a group of ghosts sitting around a small stone table drinking tea."

"That's what you thought ghosts did in their tombs?"

"Seven or eight remember? I was only seven, maybe eight."

He smiled down at her. "What happened after the disappointment faded."

"My parents found me reading the plaques of the dearly departed, and my mom gave me a lecture about disturbing the dead, and my dad agreed with her every word while at the same time praising my lockpicking skills and encouraging me to keep practicing. It was a lecture full of mixed messages."

"I'm sorry I didn't get to meet your parents,"

Christopher said. "After today, I feel like I would have liked to have known them."

"You would have. My mother would have loved you and your damsels-in-distress soft spot." She looked out over the expanse of dark headstones so he wouldn't catch the moisture gathering in her eyes or the tension in her jaw as she held back the unexpected tears.

She hadn't thought about any of this stuff in a long time. She knew, when she started this day, that she'd be opening herself to all the memories again. Letting all the good times return along with the ever-present ache of missing her parents. She'd even known what sharing this with Christopher would mean.

She just hadn't expected the tears.

They walked in silence for a few moments, the night closing in around them. In the distance, she could hear cars rumbling along Queens Boulevard, but this deep into the graveyard, everything was relatively quiet. Just the shooshing of wind through the scattered trees and a hush that felt appropriate to the setting.

When she had better control of her emotions, she said, "The tomb is where we're headed, if you hadn't guessed. That's where my father would have stored his treasures. Someplace we'd all know and remember, but not directly associated with us in any real way. And not a place likely to be broken into or even opened."

"No new family members being interred?"

"Most of that family line is gone. It was an older tomb. We researched it when we got back from the cemetery because I wanted to know who the ghosts would have been if I'd seen them. And my parents indulged me."

It had set up a pattern for her life, too. When curious, she looked things up. She didn't always find *all* the information. Sometimes the information was hidden or not available—like pictures of Christopher and his brothers weren't available anywhere—but she'd learned how to find a lot. And she really loved the research part of her job. She liked learning things.

A habit of curiosity her parents had encouraged.

"We ended up with a whole family genealogy and history," she said with a smile. Like we were researching our own ancestors. I felt quite close to the Bravermans after all that research."

She nodded ahead. Just to the left of the road and back a row or two, the little gray stone temple-shaped tomb, with its flat roof and front columns. As an adult, she realized the "house" did look more like an ancient Greek temple with those columns and the stepped decorations around the roof, but she still thought of it as a house like she had as a kid.

It wasn't a particularly elaborate tomb, despite the temple-like construction. But it was still pretty, with a set of stone steps up to the thick, rectangular wooden door, and urns bracketing the stairs that held small, evergreen bushes. Someone had decorated the bushes for the holiday with little winking white lights powered by solar batteries. The lights were dim, but sparkly.

Myra did like sparkles.

She stood at the foot of the stairs, looking at the wooden door, memories of the last time she'd picked that lock flooding her. Christopher remained quietly at her side, a steady and warm presence on the icy cold night.

Finally, she handed him back the large box with all her treasures in it and pulled her lockpicks out of her inner vest pocket. "Time to collect dad's treasure."

TWELVE

The inside of the tomb was small, tiny really. No room for Christopher to follow her in for sure. So he waited just outside as she stepped over the threshold past the wooden door she'd opened. As she put her lockpicks back into the inner pocket in her vest, she pulled out a penlight to studied the pitch-black space.

It was a lot smaller inside than she remembered from her childhood. But then, she was a lot larger now. A series of plaques lined the walls, memorials to the Braverman ancestors who'd passed on. The air inside was cold, almost as cold as it was outside, but dry with a musty smell that was hard to describe. Christopher probably smelled the bodies. She'd never been sure if there were bodies buried beneath the stone floor of the tomb or ashes from cremation behind the plaques. That hadn't been something she'd researched when looking at the family history if this tomb. All she'd known was there were no ghosts.

There were still no ghosts. Not the Braverman ghosts anyway.

The ghost of memories did haunt the place for her, though. But they were the good kind of ghost memories. The kind that made her smile softly.

She swung the penlight around, hunting around the floor, the flat ceiling above, looking for her father's treasure. She didn't *think* he'd have hidden it behind one of the plaques, but also, if some Braverman ancestor did step forward to be buried here, he wouldn't have wanted the cemetery caretakers to find the treasure.

So where would he have left it.

There was a small cubby at the very back of the tomb, an inset in the wall with a little statue of a saint, or maybe it was the Virgin Mary. It glowed faintly white when she swung her light across it. She remembered that from her one and only other visit inside the tomb, thinking at first it was one of the ghosts and then being disappointed when it wasn't.

Ducking to keep her head from brushing the low ceiling, she went closer, studied the statue. It seemed a little crooked in its nook.

"See anything?" Christopher asked from the door.

"Not sure yet. Maybe." She gently touched the statue, pushed it a little. It moved.

She got close enough to run her light over all the details of the statue near the base of the nook, and after a moment, smiled. Then she pulled the little statue forward, opening a secret panel in the wall behind it.

Her father must have installed that somehow because she couldn't imagine why the Bravermans would include something like a secret hidden nook in their crypt. Unless they wanted to hide some sort of wealth from graverobbers. But Myra figured the other Braverman family members would be more likely to retrieve any valuables left in the tomb before strange graverobbers might come looking.

She flicked her penlight's narrow beam into the hidden cavity. It danced over a patch of dark velvet, the color impossible to really see with just the penlight. She reached in and slowly pulled out the package. A thick package, wrapped in velvet.

"Found something," she said.

She ran her light over the interior of the hidey

hole again, just in case she'd missed something. It wasn't a large space and only went back about a foot. Still, she reached in a felt around. Nothing else hidden that she could detect. But then, she was pretty sure the velvet-wrapped box was all her father had left here.

Outside, Christopher stepped back to give her room, and she handed him the new box so she could relock the tomb. When she turned back, he was standing at the base of the two stairs, which brought her closer to his height. He was still a head taller her than her, but she was closer now. He was staring at her, not either of the boxes he held, and his concern was obvious in the creases between his brow.

"Why are you worried?" she asked, taking the new box back from him.

"What if it's not what you think? What if your father led you on a wild goose chase?"

"You're worried I'll be devastated and upset after everything we did tonight."

"I am."

"I won't be. The adventure of the hunt was as much the present my father left me as anything. There could be a handful of old bills in this box and I'd be okay with it. But I know what's in here. It's not old bills."

"No," said a new voice. An unfortunately remembered one. From earlier that day. "It's my boss's stolen property. And we're here to get it back."

THIRTEEN

C hristopher stepped in front of Myra before she could stop him, blocking her almost entirely from view where she still stood on the tomb steps. She glanced around his arm to assess their situation.

Phone-Guy from the Staten Island train platform and his gray puffer jacketed friend stood about a hundred feet away, with a dozen or so headstones between them and her and Christopher. They stood right next to a large obelisk headstone that could serve as cover, but they weren't behind it at the moment. Out in the open. With their guns.

Guns again. Argh.

"Nothing that belongs to anyone but my family is in here," she said. "Nothing that's valuable to your boss is here. I don't know how many times I have to say that." She scowled. "How the hell did you find us?"

Queens was a long way from Staten Island. And she and Christopher had been flying, and been all over Manhattan all afternoon and evening. They couldn't have followed them.

Phone-Guy shrugged. "Slipped a tracker into your boyfriend's pocket."

Would that work when he shifted and did the fog thing that took his clothes with it? Except for his pants and shoes, everything else had magically disappeared when he'd shifted with that fog. She couldn't image any kind of tracking device surviving that. Or that Christopher wouldn't have noticed somehow.

"You never got close enough to me to plant anything," Christopher said, his voice very deep and low. He handed the second box with all her treasures in it back to her, but didn't take his gaze off the thugs.

Myra scrambled to take both boxes, then set them on the ground at her back, near the tomb door so she'd have her hands free for… Whatever happened next.

When she faced the thugs again, Phone-Guy was grinning at Christopher, and Puffer Jacket was smirking at her.

"Remember helping that woman carry her stroller up the stairs?" Phone-Guy said.

Myra wanted to groan. Shit. Christopher had gotten into trouble *again* trying to help someone. The poor man was going to kick himself for that.

"Not the pregnant woman herself," Phone-Guy said, probably at some look on Christopher's face hinting that more explanation might prevent a stream of fire from the dragon's mouth. "She was just the distraction. And don't worry, she got paid. Good distraction. Makes it easier to sneak up behind someone and brush past without them noticing."

Christopher patted his pants pockets and pulled out a small circular plastic tracker from one of his back pockets. Phone-Guy smirked. Christopher crushed the tracker between his fingers, the plastic and electronics crumbling to near dust as it dropped to the ground.

Phone-Guy didn't flinch. Myra did.

In front of her, she could *feel* the anger pumping off Christopher. Waves of heat washing over her, as hot as an actual furnace. He was fully dressed, having returned to his clothes after shifting his wings away once they'd landed at the cemetery. And yet she could still feel so much heat from him, she was a little afraid his clothes were going to combust.

She wanted to touch his arm, to assure him everything was okay, but she was worried she'd get burnt if she did.

Looking around his big body, she gave the Phone-Guy and Puffer Jacket a head shake. "You two have made a rather serious miscalculation here. A mistake that's gonna cost you. But if you leave now and just forget about all this, you'll probably survive. Maybe. Depends on how easy you make it for a dragon to find you."

Christopher let out that growling hiss sound that meant someone was in serious trouble. A sound that didn't bode well for Phone-Guy and Puffer Jacket's survival.

"My boss hasn't waited all these years to get his stuff back for nothing," Phone-Guy said. "We're taking that." He nodded at the ground behind Myra where both boxes sat. "We'll take them both. And you might survive the process if you cooperate."

Myra stepped back closer to the boxes and shook her head. "No. These aren't anything your boss wants. But they are important to me. You can't have either box."

She started calculating the best escape, where they could go to get cover from those guns, find a place open enough for Christopher to shift and get them airborne but not so open they'd get shot.

Normally, when Myra planned a heist, she had backup plans on her backup plans. Some of those were a little amorphous and she had to calculate contingencies and make things up as she went, but there was usually some knowledge and forethought put into even the amorphous contingency plans.

She hadn't made one here. She hadn't thought these guys could have tracked them. She hadn't even considered that they might be good enough to slip a tracker on Christopher even before she'd met with Harry. That they'd know enough about Christopher to know something like the pregnant woman needing help up slippery stairs with her stroller would attract Christopher's attention.

Whatever their boss wanted back, he was very very serious about it. But Myra *knew* what she'd recovered from the tomb had nothing to do with that. She knew what was in the new box. And it wasn't something that was valuable to anyone but her.

So she didn't have a contingency plan in place for this. She knew this cemetery from her youth but hadn't been here in more than a decade. The layout of the place scrolled across her mind as she searched for options, but the details were fuzzy after so many years, making the planning harder.

All the mental effort she put into trying to figure a way out of all this…

She should have known better.

Christopher was truly pissed. As angry as she'd ever seen him. Maybe even angrier. He might have been this angry when she'd been hit by a wizard bolt and went tumbling down an elevator shaft, but she was unconscious so she couldn't say for sure.

All she knew was that in this moment, he was angry enough that the heat coming off him felt like fire. And the scent of sulfur was getting stronger. And there was even a faint glow of purple fog swirling in the air around him that wasn't obvious in the dark but was starting to obscure his legs.

If he shifted to his full dragon form right in front of her, would any of the nearby headstones survive? Would the Braverman tomb?

She started to reach for him, but the air around him was so hot it was like holding her hand over an open flame.

Her eyes wide, she looked at Phone-Guy, at Puffer Jacket. "You have about twenty seconds to get away."

Phone-Guy laughed. "He ain't gonna crisp us. He wouldn't dare. He does, he's made an enemy of my boss. And he don't want that."

"I'll take my chances," Christopher said. His voice was so deep, so guttural, he did not sound like himself. "Back against the tomb," he said, quieter. To her.

Myra didn't hesitate. She stepped as close to the tomb as she could get, tight against the door with the two boxes just beside her.

A rush of heat and sound and fire erupted from Christopher in a stream that arrowed out over the tops of the headstones.

FOURTEEN

The whole thing lasted less than a second. In that second, Myra thought she might have heard gun shots, but by the time the guns went off, it would have been much too late.

The light from Christopher's stream of fire was so intensely bright, she squeezed her eyes shut. Even like that, she knew when the fire stopped. The roaring sound cut off abruptly. The heat against her skin eased slightly. The crinkling of soil turned to glass filled in the quiet. And the stench of burnt grass and…other things, wafted through the air.

In the distance, the sounds of traffic. But nothing else.

The cemetery was very quiet.

She opened her eyes and blinked away the after-image spots.

Without her penlight, with only the ambient light from the surrounding city to show her anything, the charred lumps where Phone-Guy and Puffer Jacket had been standing were hard to see in detail. That was for the best. The details were one thing Myra was not curious about.

"I did warn them," she said quietly. She'd been unconscious the last time Christopher had crisped somebody, so she hadn't been confronted by the reality of it. Knowing someone could do something, and watching them do it were two different things.

Watching fire erupt from Christopher, even for a second, had been a terrifying reality check.

Not that she forgot he was a dragon shifter. Not that she underestimated his killing ability.

She just hadn't witnessed it before.

He turned back to her slowly, carefully, and watched her through wary eyes. There was a yellow glow this time over the blue, a glow she only saw when he was angry. That glow faded, but his eyes were still lit and bright in the nighttime. He wasn't breathing hard. The heat that had been pumping off him had eased. And the smell of sulfur was gone. Replaced by...

Sugar cookies.

Not charged bodies, though if she concentrated, that smell reached her. But if she didn't, all she got was that scent of vanilla and sugar that she sometimes got from Christopher. And it was strong enough to block out everything else. Strong enough she almost smiled. It was a pleasant, yummy smell she found hard to resist.

And she realized suddenly, that was absolutely the point.

"You smell like sugar cookies again," she said.

He blinked. That probably wasn't one of the first things he'd expected her to say in this moment.

"Do you understand why yet?" he asked quietly.

"Can't find it anywhere. Been looking since the female dragon incident."

"It's not common knowledge." He nodded. "Are you hurt?"

"Of course not. Last time you did this around me, I was in your arms and unconscious and I still wasn't hurt. Why would I be hurt standing behind you?"

"Just checking." His voice was easing back to normal. Still a bit guttural, but he sounded like himself again.

"You're worried about how I feel about all this," she guessed.

His nod was jerky and quick.

"Think it'll change the way I feel about you?"

Another jerky nod.

"But you'd do it again to protect me."

That same nod. He never once broke eye contact.

"I mean… They did have guns. And we did warn them to back off. Can't blame us that they're too stupid to recognize the danger they put themselves into." She shrugged. "Not going to look at them too closely now, though."

"Don't. You won't like it." He took a step toward her, then stopped abruptly. His hands opened and closed into fists at his side.

"You still too hot to touch?" she asked.

He shook his head. "Wasn't sure you'd want me to touch you."

Oh. Well. She closed the space between them and wrapped her arms around his waist, pressing tight against him. He was still warm, but not that furnace hot anymore.

"For the record," she said, "crisping bad people with guns pointed at us is not the kind of thing that will make me want to avoid touching you."

All his muscles seemed to relax at once, like he flowed from statue stiff into a living man as he wrapped his arms around her and brought his mouth down on hers so suddenly, she gasped. Then she sank into the kiss. There was a lot of relief there. Relief that no one had been shot. Relief that the thugs hadn't taken her father's treasure. And relief that, between them at least, this hadn't changed things.

His kiss was deep, sweeping, intense. Not bruising. But the intensity, the sheer passion of it left her breathless and hungry and dizzy. Left her wanting so much more.

Finally. Soon.

She eased back, but not enough to let any cold night air sneak in between them. Blinked up at him as he stared down at her. His breathing was as ragged as hers. She reached up and touched his cheek.

"Are *you* okay?" she asked. At least one of the guns had gone off in that second as the flame swept across the tombstones.

His arms flexed around her. "Now I am."

That brought out a soft smile. "We should get out of here. The caretakers are going to have an awful surprise in the morning."

"They'll know it was a dragon."

"But not which one. Will this cause you problems, though?"

"Not with anyone who matters." Again, his arms flexed around her.

Her heartbeat pounded a little harder, and the flutter in her stomach intensified. And really all she wanted in that moment was to get him somewhere safe and alone.

"Can we go to your place?" she asked quietly, holding his gaze.

He swept her up into his arms so fast, she got dizzy. But the move made her chuckle and she was sure that was the point.

"Wait, the boxes!" He released her reluctantly, which was sweet, and she stacked the boxes, velvet-wrapped on top, in her arms.

When she turned back to him, he swept her up again before she could gasp. Then his chest and arms flexed, a shredding of clothing across his back, and his wings spread wide behind him.

She widened her eyes up at him. "Why not just do that fog thing?"

"I'd have to let you go again, and I don't want to."

"Oh." Her heart skipped giddily in her chest. "You ruined your clothes for me."

"And for me. Like I said, I don't want to let you go. Not even long enough to take the coat off. I can replace the coat."

That heart-pounding, stomach-fluttering thing got worse. Left her breathless. Left her dizzy all over again.

She cradled the two boxes tightly in her arms and leaned in to him. She wanted to wrap herself around him and never let go either. But this would do for now.

"Let's go," she said.

He dipped and then launched into the air, his wings snapping downward and catching an air current, bringing them high, circling over Queens as they turned back toward Manhattan. Back toward his apartment.

Toward something…new.

FIFTEEN

On the flight, Christopher asked her about the velvet-wrapped box. What she intended on doing with it.

"Opening it. With you." Myra hugged her arms tighter around the two boxes. "That was always the plan. I want you to see what's in here. It's important."

Somehow, showing him this after the day they'd had seemed even more important now. For him to understand what all this meant to her. For her. It just felt, well, important.

Especially because she was quite certain somewhere in the last few months, she'd tumbled past desire and lust into something much more serious. She didn't just like Christopher. She didn't just want him. She wanted more from him than she'd ever wanted from a man.

And confronting that reality meant looking through her past.

As his feet settled onto the stone balcony of his apartment, he tightened his grip on her, as if he didn't want to set her down. She didn't mind. She wasn't in a hurry to get out of his arms either.

"You're sure about this?" he asked.

Myra nodded. "Never been more sure of anything."

He carried her toward the French doors that opened into his apartment. She'd been on this balcony with him several times. And fallen asleep here once, when she'd drifted off in a comfy lounger while they watched a movie—their first technical date—and she'd woken in a huge bed inside. Alone. And fully dressed.

The alone and dressed had felt a little unfortunate at the time but also a relief, because at that time, she hadn't been quite ready for where that step would take their relationship.

She was more than ready now. Beyond ready. Her body tingling and restless and eager. She had one more thing she needed to do, though, and it was show him what her father had left behind for her to find.

But instead of staying on the balcony to look

through the velvet-wrapped box's contents, Christopher carried her right inside. She wasn't sure if the balcony was more comfortable for him even in the winter. She hadn't asked. But it was where they spent most of their time when they were here.

This time was different. On a lot of levels.

Inside, he nudged the door closed behind him and Myra took in the apartment at night. Recessed lights flickered on automatically when they stepped inside, but the lighting was dim and comfortable after coming in from the darkness. Only bright enough to keep from tripping on anything. Not that Christopher left much around to trip on.

The back door opened onto a large living room with a double high ceiling. The air was cool, but not cold like outside. Not overly heated like a lot of New York apartments in the winter, though. She might have even found it too cool if she wasn't cradled in his very warm arms still. The floors were black marble, the furniture minimal. Just a couch and a couple of chairs, all with metal bases and stiff looking cushions. Not the sort of couch you sank into and took a nap on. Or at least, she wouldn't. But Christopher might find that solid base comfortable for naps.

She had a hard time picturing him napping on

the couch though and wondered if he ever did. That would be fun to witness for reasons she couldn't name but that made her feel a little melty inside.

There was also a wide, deep marble fireplace in front of the couch, and a huge flat-screen TV hung on the wall above the mantle-less fireplace. There wasn't a lot of art or pictures on the wall. A double-high bookshelf opposite the TV, with no ladder to reach the high shelves, and filled with mostly genre books. She'd snooped when he'd left her alone in his bed, but not too much. She'd just looked at all the obvious stuff, like his taste in fiction, which ran, somewhat ironically, to mysteries and thrillers and heist novels. Though he also had an impressive collection of Romance novels and even some literary fiction. What he didn't have, she noticed, were any fantasy books that involved dragons.

Hard to blame him for that.

A set of wide, circular metal stair near the middle back of the huge room wound up to the second floor and the huge bedroom suite. Behind the staircase, an open kitchen with shiny appliances she'd never asked if he used.

The place was spotlessly clean and pretty bare all in all. Especially for a dragon who did have a hoard somewhere around here. Or somewhere.

He'd never disclosed the location of his hoard and she hadn't gone looking for it. Especially after learning that him voluntarily showing her his hoard…meant something important. It was something dragons only did with their mates. When she'd learned that, she'd tamped down her curiosity and had left that secret a secret.

She hadn't thought deeply about why until now. Now she realized it was because she wanted that voluntary tour one day. And she didn't want to spoil that or make assumptions.

The same reason she wanted to voluntarily show him *her* treasures, even if the velvet wrapped box didn't really count as a hoard. It was the closest she came to one.

"Want anything to drink?" he asked, still cradling her in his arms. It was almost like he forgot he was carrying her sometimes. Like holding her this way was so natural and easy, he forgot to set her down.

She really didn't mind and still wasn't in a hurry to leave his arms, but she patted his shoulders and he let her legs ease to the ground. "Would take a tea if it's not too much trouble."

He released her—very reluctantly, which was gratifying—and went to the kitchen while she went to the couch to sit down. He had a metal and marble-topped coffee table in front of the couch with nothing on it. No magazines or nicknacks or plants. The minimal space was nice, but she thought he needed at least one or two plants. And she wondered about the place because it felt... temporary even though this was always where they went when they needed a private place.

The bedroom hadn't felt temporary, she remembered. But those were thoughts for later.

From the kitchen, Christopher said, "Fireplace on." And a row of flames flashed up across a gas line at the base of the hearth, warming the room almost immediately.

"Fancy," she said.

"I don't use it often, but I thought it might be cold in here for you."

"Thanks." She set the velvet box on the coffee table and the box she'd gotten from Harry, which contained all their other finds from the scavenger hunt, under the table out of the way. Then she shifted on the couch so she could watch him putter in the kitchen. That felt so intimate, almost too intimate, watching him opening and closing cabinets, putting an electric kettle on to boil. All the little manual steps to making a cup of tea. Unlike his casually voice-activated fireplace, this he did by hand.

He brought her a cup of peppermint tea, which reminded her of candy canes, and that reminded her they were only two days away from Christmas, less now since it was after midnight. She took a few sips of her tea before setting the mug gently on the coffee table and picking up the velvet wrapped box, carefully unwrapping the soft material—which turned out to be a dark shade of purple that strangely reminded her of Christopher's scales.

Beneath the velvet was a brass box the size of a long, narrow mailing box, but shaped to have a flap over it that made it look like an oversized envelop or one of those file folders that people in offices used. This was all metal, though, and the tab that held the flap shut was a pretty, decorative brass rose. Her mother's favorite flower.

She set her hand on the top of the brass flap, over the small rose tab. "This was something very precious to my father, and very important. But, like I said, it wouldn't be important to anyone else. Except me and my parents. Harry might have found this important if he'd known what was really here. But as my dad's best friend, he never asked, and my dad wouldn't have told."

"You don't have to share this with me if it's too personal," he said quietly. "Even after everything today."

"No. I want to. That's the point. The reason we did this today. I want to."

He softly caressed his fingertips over the hand she had set on the box. "Only if you're sure."

She smiled, her gaze on his huge hand so gently caressing the back of hers, his thumb brushing her skin in a reassuring gesture that was both soothing and also made her stomach fluttering worse.

Giving herself a little shake, she moved her hand and he pulled his back so she could open the flap.

She considered the little rose tab, a small button that needed to be pushed to open the flap. No locks here, though. Just a gentle push and the flap sprung upward a little so she could fold it back on hinges that didn't resist the movement, even after all this time.

She said, "You know how your father won't allow pictures of any of the royal family?"

Christopher nodded, a gesture she had to look up to see.

"I sort of waved that off, thought it was a bit odd, but whatever. Except... My dad had a similar policy when I was growing up. No pictures. Not even among ourselves."

"Why?"

"He didn't want any of the people he worked with to have pictures of us. He even went so far as to buy a magical charm he would set up around wherever we lived so people couldn't take pictures of us while we were at home. He didn't want any of his enemies to figure out what we looked like, at least not in images that could be easily passed around."

"Makes a kind of sense."

"He was trying to preserve our privacy and safety. Took me a bit to realize that's what your father was doing for you and your brothers."

"That and he's a controlling bastard who wanted to ensure he kept the spotlight."

She snorted. "Yeah, that sounds right, too. Still. The ban on pictures of the royal family has helped you keep some sort of anonymity. Even if you can't hide that you're a dragon shifter."

There was a pause, and then he said, "I suppose it's helped. Did your father's dictate help you?"

"I suppose it did. Honestly, I rarely thought about it. We just didn't have pictures lying around, and it never really occurred to me that this was a thing that should occur to me. But..." She glanced down at the box. "But my mother was sentimental. And my father more so because of her. So sometimes we did take pictures. Sometimes. Sometimes, my father even kept them." She met Christopher's gaze. "I haven't seen them in ten years. I barely remember their faces because time does that. I can hear my mother's voice still sometimes. And I definitely hear my dad's voice if I'm taking too long to pick a lock."

Christopher smiled at that.

"But I haven't seen them in a long time." She patted the brass box. "This is our treasure." She laid the flap back against the couch, revealing the interior of the thin rectangular box, and the small pile of pictures inside.

Some were polaroids from way back in the day. Some were pictures from a roll of film that her dad had processed himself so no one would have access to the negatives. Some were printouts from a later digital camera only a year before they died. Pictures of them together. Pictures of her opening a present. Pictures of a sunny outing to Coney Island or the zoo. Smiling.

There were a few of just her parents, looking at each other. The love obvious even in the shot. One she even remembered taking during one of her dad's weak moments when he wanted to preserve something. There was a shot of her and mom in front of the Bryant Park Christmas tree. And another on the Staten Island Ferry. She couldn't remember why they'd been on the ferry that particular time. Probably going to see Harry.

And speaking of... There were a few photos of her dad and Harry together. A couple with her mom, dad, and Harry, all hamming it up for the camera. One with her mom holding Myra as a baby, and her dad and Harry standing on either side, looking terrified and delighted at once.

There weren't as many as she imagined other people gathered over a lifetime, but there were enough. Enough to spark memories. Enough to feel thing she hadn't allowed herself to in years.

Enough to see them again.

She touched the image of Harry standing beside her mom and dad when she was a baby. "Ten years was maybe a little too long," she murmured.

"Why did you stay away so long?" Christopher said quietly. "I mean, I get why you weren't ready for the pictures. But why did you stay away from Harry for so long?"

She shook her head, sighing. "At first… After my parents died, I got a bit…reckless in my thieving. Took the kinds of risks I wouldn't normally. I was… It was like I *wanted* to get caught. I thought, if I did, and I ended up in jail like my father used to off and on, I didn't want Harry to feel like he had to bail me out, look after me, take heat because of me. The way he'd done for my dad all those years. He'd done enough. I didn't want him taking on those same…chores with me." She shrugged. "Once the grief lifted enough to see what I was doing, I was embarrassed to go back. Then I thought I might not be welcome. And then it just became a habit. You get used to being on your own. You get used to being alone."

"So why now? As you said, ten years is a long time."

She glanced up at him from under her lashes, knowing what she was doing here and still nervous. "That thing with the female dragon, with Jasmin... That left me shaky. Left me thinking about my own mortality in a way I don't usually."

"You jump off the side of buildings regularly. Your mortality never crosses your mind?"

She grinned. "Nope. I know what I'm doing when I do that. I have an element of control over the amount of risk I'm taking. I love risks."

He snorted, a sound half humor, half groan.

"What can I say? It comes with my innate skills, I think. My dad was the same way. But taking risks where I've calculated the odds and know what I'm getting into is one thing. That's a rush. It's fun. Having an unpredictable female dragon somewhere out there who not only knows who I am, but maybe doesn't like me so much is something else. And it's not like I haven't made some enemies over the years. But none of them quite like her. None of my enemies could lay waste to the entire island of Manhattan in a few sweeps and then go take a nap. That's next level spooky. So, yeah, I've been thinking about my life. And the possibility of my death."

"And you didn't want to die before seeing Harry again and doing...this." He gestured to the pictures spread out across the couch between them and in her lap.

But she knew that gesture took in their entire day, the last twenty-four hours of the scavenger hunt.

"Exactly. I didn't want to die with Harry thinking...thinking I didn't remember him or think about him. And I didn't want to die leaving the last thing my dad ever did for me unfinished." She glanced down at the pictures in her lap. "I didn't want to die without seeing them again." She blinked up at Christopher. "And I didn't want to die before I showed them to you. So someone else besides me and Harry could...remember them. Maybe long past when I die. Someone else will have known they existed."

Christopher reached across the space between them and cupped her cheek. "I'm honored. I'll remember them. We have an accord."

She smiled a little even as tears she *never* shed pricked at her eyes. "You said that to that dragon in Chicago, Archer. Sounds very formal."

"It is. It's a formal giving of our word. All dragons take that phrase as an unbreakable oath. We don't say it lightly."

The sentimental ache in her heart flipped over to something else, something different but just as strong.

"Thank you." She rubbed her face against his palm. "I knew you'd understand."

And wasn't that just amazing.

Sixteen

Gently, Myra put the photos back into the brass box, smiling as she got flashes of her mom or dad's smiling faces. These joined *her* "hoard" now. Not that she called her small treasure collection a hoard since she wasn't a dragon. Still, she kept a few things, special things, in a safe place. And this would be stored with them.

But in the meantime, there was something else she needed to do tonight. Or this morning since it was closer to sunrise than to midnight now.

She set the box on the marbled topped coffee table, next to her forgotten and cooling cup of peppermint tea. Christopher blinked at her when she took his mug, now empty, and set it on the coffee table, too.

He didn't say anything, but he watched her through narrow eyes.

"Why do you smell like sugar cookies to me sometimes?" she asked. "Everyone but me seems to know the significance."

She'd taken off her coat earlier, when they'd separated so he could make tea, and had draped it across the back of the couch. Christopher had dropped the last shreds of his coat and shirt somewhere near the kitchen. He'd kicked off his shoes almost the minute they stepped into his apartment. She wondered if the cool marble felt good on his feet. The heat from the gas fire washed over the couch, leaving the marble here warmer as she kicked off her own shoes, shoving them under the coffee table.

Still watching her warily, Christopher said, "Dragons can do that sometimes. Adjusted our scent. It's...biology. To put...someone at ease."

"Is it in your control?"

"Not entirely. Somewhat. But not entirely. Like I said, it's biology."

"Why sugar cookies? Does every dragon smell that way when they're trying to put someone at ease?"

"We'll smell like whatever the person we're... We'll smell like something they love."

"I do love sugar cookies." She stood and faced him.

In that moment, he looked up at her. He was so tall she rarely had this perspective, being able to look at him from this angle. She liked it, the way his expression softened, the way the angle of his mouth was just right.

He faced her more fully, and she nudged his thighs apart so she could step closer. His hand came up to her hips automatically. The same way he caught her when she jumped into his arms before a flight. Like that's where his hands were always supposed to be. His fingers flexed against her, digging into her skin as she got close enough he had to tip his head back. Not all that far. Even sitting down, he was still almost as tall as her, but she did like this unique angle.

"Thank you for showing me your family," he said quietly. "For showing me your memories."

"It was important. To me. That you.. saw me. Saw where I came from." She wasn't prepared to say why yet. It was enough to even admit she wanted him to see her.

"I do." His voice was a quiet whisper in the huge room.

The fireplace at her back was a line of warmth that felt almost cool compared to Christopher's heat. But he wasn't so hot that she couldn't touch. This was the kind of warmth that made her want to get closer, want to snuggle up against him all night.

His blue eyes glittered and a faint purple glow rose from the depths, lighting his eyes. His expression, intent on her, hungry as he scanned her face, made her heart pound hard for all the right reasons.

Finally, she leaned down, leaned in, and settled her mouth over his. A kiss that started in a gentle coming together. A brush of lips. A sealing of understanding.

But before one breath and the next, that kiss erupted, intensity and need washing through her in a flash. She angled her head, deepened the kiss... or maybe he deepened it. She didn't know and didn't really care. Just needed his mouth on hers, his tongue tangled with her, his breath against her cheek, his hands tight on her body.

He moved his hands from her hips, to hug around her, banded her close, so as much of her body as they could manage pressed against him. Not quite enough, though. Not quite right.

She straddled him on the couch, climbing up and settling on his lap, her legs bracketing his thighs. Better better. She rocked against him, felt the press of his hard cock against her and moaned into his mouth.

Sensation rushed through her. The feel of his chest hard against her breasts, the muscles of his shoulder flexing under her fingers. All skin now. No scales. The feel of all that muscle, bunched and tight and hard against her was dizzying, satisfying like cracking a particularly tricky lock.

Hers.

In this moment. This night. He was hers. She felt it in his every sinew, in his every flex and groan. When she ground down against him and he growled. When he tightened the band of his arms around her back, dragging her up closer, higher against his chest so he could devour her mouth.

She wasn't sure who got her vest, shirt, and bra off. They somehow fumbled the clothing off together, but she was so high on his kiss, she barely noticed. Until her bare skin touched his. And a deep, thrilling satisfaction washed over her. Yes. She'd wanted this sensation for a long time now. Since meeting him. Since that very first kiss.

The rough scrape of his chest hair against her peaked nipples. The heat of his skin seeping directly into hers without any barrier. Her chest flattened against his. His hands splayed against her back, so large they nearly spanned the full width. His breath against her neck as he kissed along her jaw, down her throat. Her breathing heavy and deep and erratic at once.

Restlessly, she ground down against him, savoring his moan. Loving the way his fingers flexed into her skin. She felt his restraint, a tension in him that resisted release. Like he was afraid to hurt her. After watching him easily move an eight-hundred-pound bell around that night, she was grateful for the consideration. But she couldn't imagine him hurting her. Not on purpose. Not physically. She suspected he'd cut off his own arm before hurting her.

And the thought that he was so protective of her, not just any damsel in distress, but *her* in particular, seeped through her like warmed honey, leaving a deliciously deep sense of melting belonging, of delight and satisfaction and a thrilling sort of fear.

She clutched him tight as he stood abruptly, one hand wrapped under her ass to keep her in place. The change in position made her gasp, then she chuckled, because she loved that sudden, shocking move as much as she liked having her legs wrapped around his waist.

She did want to get her pants off soon, though, so there was no longer any barrier between her legs and his bare waist.

His lips still clinging to hers, or moving away only to taste more of her skin, he walked her to the wide, circular metal staircase that led up to the second level of his apartment. To his bed. She sank into his kisses, trusting him to navigate the stairs without dropping her or hurting himself, though the thought that he was going to had her heartbeat hammering. She clung tighter to him when he released the hand around her back to hold the railing, keeping one solid arm under her ass to hold her securely.

The climb was a series of rapid assents and pausing to sink into a deep kiss before he practically leapt up the next few steps. And when he finally reached the second-floor landing, she was so restless to have the rest of their close off, she was grinding against him, taking herself close to orgasm before she'd even gotten her pants off! The feel of his large hand spanning her ass didn't help.

She didn't notice them crossing the space between the bed and the stairs. Most of the second floor was his bedroom, with a huge bathroom and closet, but mostly open. That meant fewer doors in the way. That meant fewer barriers between them and the giant bed. Not that she would have noticed. He could have plowed through a solid wall and she wouldn't have noticed the dust settling on her. She was too caught up in the feel of his mouth under hers. She had her arms wrapped around his head now, kissing him so eagerly, so deeply, her world in that moment was him.

A change of position, the feel of his leg coming up under her as he climbed up onto his bed. She still clung to him, her legs firmly around his waist, and didn't relax until he'd settled them both down onto the mattress.

Almost as soon as her legs left his waist, he started kissing his way down her body, across her neck, nipping lightly at the skin between her neck and shoulder, making her arch up under him. One of his huge hands engulfed her small breast, gently cupping her in heat, her nipple rubbing against his palm. He flicked his thumb over her nipple, and she gasped, arching into his touch again.

Her entire body felt electrified, her nerves close to the surface. His lips gliding over her skin as he moved lower left a blazing trail of heated tingles in their wake. When he took one of her nipples into his mouth and sucked gently, she felt the tug all the way to her core. Already dangerously close to coming, that pressure pushed her even closer to the edge. And she still wasn't even out of her fucking pants.

Fumbling at her chunky heeled boots, she managed to kicked and wiggle them off, barely aware of the dull thud of them dropping to the rug that spread under the bed. Her pants and underwear were not so easy to wiggle out of when Christopher's big body was in the way as he continued exploring her skin with his mouth. He was taking his sweet time about the process, and that was both electrifying and frustrating.

But when his lips slid down the side of her ribs, along her waist, the combination of being overly sensitive and him hitting a lot of nerves in that pass made her thinking short circuit. She moaned and wrapped her legs around him again, desperate for some relief, pressure where she needed it most to relieve the building tension.

He trailed his lips farther down, over her belly, lower to the edge of her pants. She was wearing her usual black yoga pants, the kind of pants that didn't get in the way when she had to, say, scale a building. They were definitely in the way now, though, when she wanted to scale Christopher.

The good thing about her leggings, though, was that they were very easy to pull off. And fortunately, Christopher didn't waste time doing just that, taking her underwear with the leggings in one sweep. Though he did it slowly enough to make Myra whimper. Sliding the material down her legs in inches, kissing skin as he exposed it. Dropping licks and gentle bites along her thighs, the inside of her knees, her calves, a gentle kiss on her ankle as he tugged the rest of her clothing all the way off.

With that barrier gone, she reached for him, wanting his skin against hers again. He obliged but again slowly, sliding kisses up her legs, spreading her legs this time, and when he nibbled the inside of her thigh, licked his way higher along that sensitive skin, she bowed up, her jaw tight as the sensations made her want to scream and moan and come. And she could do none of that because it was all so much, so good, so deliciously electric. But when his mouth finally, found her slick wet heat and settled over her, licked a line over her and into her, flicked her swollen clit, Myra found her voice, moaning and panting his name.

She was so on fire, so sensitive and ready, she couldn't even open her eyes. She wanted to see him, to watch him, but her body wasn't entirely in her control in that moment. Her eyes stayed firmly shut, all her focus on that single point of building tension and sensation so perfect she couldn't even think. She bunched one hand in the sheets, another grasped his hair. He held her hips down as he pleasured her, his huge hands gentle but firm, and that only intensified the lush delight of his mouth on her clit.

Everything felt so good, so overwhelming and viciously perfect, she wanted it to last forever, and yet knew she couldn't take this level of sensation much longer. She wanted to hold back the building tide to enjoy his mouth and tongue on her as long as possible. But as long as possible wasn't very. Her body wound tight, so tight she knew she'd scream soon. Another flick of his tongue, a long firm suck…

And she fell. Tumbled completely. Free falling in an explosion of sensations that lit her body up and left her shivering and shaking. The echo of her scream filling the huge bedroom.

When she was able to finally open her eyes, finally look down at him, he was watching her, his eyes with that faint purple glow in them, and he was holding her close. Catching her as she came back down from the heights he'd taken her.

Just like she knew he always would.

That look in his eyes, the satisfaction and smugness, made her shake her head. "Get up here. I want more."

"Greedy," he said, his voice deep and graveling, rubbing over her already sensitive skin and making her shiver. "Good thing for you I like greedy and am *very* happy to follow that order."

She grinned. Then pointed at his pants. "Off."

Removing his pants went faster than hers but it still felt like too long because he wasn't touching her while he did. Then he was on the bed with her again, his warm body sliding up along hers. He was just so big he engulfed her and she loved it. She much of him to explore and wrap herself around. Which she did. Kissing every inch of his skin she could reach. His waist was surprisingly sensitive when she kissed him there. The thick muscle over his hip bones obsessed her. The thick ridge of his erection impossible to resist. And the sounds of his hissing breaths and groaning growls did make her exactly what he'd accused her of. Greedy. Greedy for more of those sounds, greedy for the taste of him on her tongue, greedy for the hard feel of his muscles under her sensitive finger tips. The textures and contrasts, smooth, hard, some roughness from the hair on his legs, at the base of his cock.

When she slipped the head of his erection between her lips and got a satisfying growl from him, she dipped lower, sliding her tongue and lips over him, savoring his taste and feel in her mouth as much as the sound of his panting pleasure. She wanted more. All. Everything that was him. And she wanted it all at once.

She was so focused on his taste, she gasped in

surprise when he suddenly lifted her up over his chest, so fast she didn't even have a chance to protest until her face was in his. "I was having fun," she pouted.

"So was I," he said, his voice so rough and deep it barely sounded like him. "But I've wanted you for so long, I don't want to come in your mouth. Not this time anyway. I want to be buried in your heat, feel that tight wet pussy around my cock when I come."

She shivered at the description. "Sounds perfect. Let's do that."

His chuckle vibrated against her breasts.

He nuzzled her ear and neck, making her hum in the back of her throat, then said, "How much did you learn about dragon shifters and sex in all that research of yours?"

For reasons that seemed ridiculous at that moment, she felt a wash of heat crawling up her face. Given she was naked and sprawled on top of him and had just had his cock in her mouth, being embarrassed now felt weird.

"Enough to know condoms are unnecessary," she said.

Dragons controlled a lot of their bodily functions, including their ability to reproduce. Dragons didn't have kids on accident. They had kids because they chose to. Coming didn't release active sperm unless they wanted it to. They *did* have non-reproductive orgasms, a fact she'd be weirdly relieved to learn. And humans and dragon shifters didn't exchange STDs, so protection against those things weren't necessary either.

They were, almost, the perfect lovers in that way. Which was one of the many reasons humans tended to stand in awe of dragon shifters.

The only draw back to taking a dragon lover, so she'd read, was the possessiveness they often displayed. With a dragon, jealousy and possessiveness was fire-breathing dangerous. And a lot of humans found that possessiveness oppressive. Even scary. So it complicated taking a dragon lover. Complicated things more if you had a child with one of them.

Myra wasn't looking for kids any time soon. Maybe never, but she wasn't set on that. She was still getting used to the idea that she wanted someone in her life the way she wanted Christopher in her life. The idea of him getting jealous and possessive and losing some of what made him so attractive to her had been a little off-putting. But in the end, worth the risk.

This was Christopher after all.

She rose up enough to look him in the eyes. The purple glow covering his blue eyes was fascinating and she got caught in the bejeweled play of lights for a moment before giving herself a little shake. The gesture made him groan, and his hands on her back clenched tighter.

"Probably should have discussed this before being distracted by all the naked skin," she whispered.

"Probably." The rough sound of his voice sent another shiver through her and she slid down on him a little, nudge herself closer to the head of his erection.

He sucked in a deep breath, closed his eyes briefly. When his eyes flickered open, the purple was more intense. And the scent of sugar cookies wove through the other scents of sweat and musk and sex in the room. She smiled at that.

"I will take care of you," he said. "And I will not go anywhere you don't want to. In anything."

She wasn't sure he could control all the things enough to keep those promises. But the mere fact that he'd try burned away any residual worries that might have remained under the surface of her lust. She slid forward again to capture his mouth in a kiss she hoped conveyed all she was feeling. She didn't have words for most of this. She'd never felt like this before. But she hoped he'd understand even that with her kiss.

Then she moved down again, until his cock nudged against her heat. His sharply drawn breath filled her with satisfaction. But not nearly as much satisfaction as the slow slide down onto his cock, the way he filled her, stretched her, inch by delicious, thick inch. And he fit her perfectly. Not too big, despite their size difference—a possibility that had crossed her mind, but turned out dragons could control this to an extent too, adjusting to their partners so they were both pleased with the way everything fit together. She wasn't sure how much of that adjusting Christopher did in that moment, but she did know the way they fit was perfect for her and she wanted more. All.

She dropped her hips back hard for the last few inches and that sharp move brought a groan from both of them. A moment when she could feel all of him, felt so connected to this one man she wondered how they'd ever *not* been connected this way. Only a moment's pause though, before the restlessness, the need to move took over.

She rocked against him, rode the length of him, held his intense gaze until the sheer feel of fucking him swamped her senses and she closed her eyes. Didn't help her escape the intensity, though. The build of tension through her rose fast, surprising since she'd just had an orgasm not so long ago. Their position ensured he hit her in just the right spots, sending her spiraling upward, everything tight and desperate and urgent.

The sounds of their pants, their groans, the slap of skin against skin, the sweat that slicked between their bodies, all of the heat and friction… Myra held out for as long as possible, wanting to feel all this for as long as possible, this thrill of climbing so high, so fast, the rush of it. But then Christopher moved his hips a little, and that hit a spot inside that was like touching an electrical socket, sending so much sensation through her, she lost her bid for control.

Dropping off the side of a building was nothing to this fall, and she went with a shattered cry that echoed with his as she felt him pulse with her, in her. A moment of shivering, perfect breaking apart. Together.

Then she sank against his big chest, curled herself around him, his arms tightly banding around her waist. And she felt the security of his hold again, catching her as she sank back to earth. Just the way she knew he would.

"Worth the wait," she muttered into his neck. And grinned when his rusty chuckle bounced against her.

She wasn't exactly sure where they went from here and what this meant in the long run, but she knew she didn't want to be anywhere else but right here, right now. Nothing had ever felt quite this perfect, quite this…right.

And for now, that was all she needed. For now, this was all she wanted. The rest would work itself out.

For maybe the first time in her life, Myra was happy to go into something risky without a plan.

Freefalling.

Because Christopher was there to catch her.

THANK YOU

Thank you so much for reading this holiday themed episode in the Dragon Thief series! I hope you enjoyed reading THE SCAVENGER JOB as much as I enjoyed writing it. Since I think of this series along the same lines as a TV series, and because I've spent so much time watching British and Irish TV, I absolutely couldn't resist doing a Christmas/Holiday episode. This seems to be a staple of most of those shows, especially the older ones, and I wanted to follow that pattern. Plus, it seemed like an ideal time for this kind of sentimental story.

And for my Romance readers, I promised you actual burn eventually in this slow burn romance. Hope that payoff was (cough) satisfying. That part was fun to write, too! About time, right?

But the story is not done! There is much more Dragon Thief to come. Starting early in 2025 with the first book in Season Two, THE CROWN OF KINGSHIP JOB. This season of the series will change things up a little, adding a team to Myra and Christopher's adventures. We'll see a little more of Myra's history, including meeting one of her biggest rivals in the thief world. And we might even see what the dragon king had in mind for Christopher before Myra came along to ruin things by making Christopher smell like sugar cookies. *grin*

There is *so much more*. And I don't have a network looming in the background waiting to cancel this show. LOL. I'm really looking forward to writing these stories and bringing them to readers. I also really hope you've enjoyed the journey so far.

To keep up to date on my releases, events, and all the news, please consider joining my monthly readers newsletter. You'll get all the news and events, discount codes to my store, occasional excerpts and cover reveals, and sometimes a free story. All new subscribers get two exclusive newsletter stories, one is a short story in my Tiger Shifters paranormal romance series, and the other is a novella in my Cary Redmond urban fantasy series.

If you'd prefer, you can see all my new and upcoming releases at my store. I also have a fun new section at the store called The Café at KatSimonsBooks—because bookstores need coffee shops, right?—where I post free short stories twice a month and have specific merchandise related to the Café. Eventually, the Café will have its own newsletter, but at the moment, if you join the store newsletter, you'll get updates when new stories are available or new merchandise is added.

In addition to these more interactive options, you can get the latest news at my website, or you can also follow my author page at BookBub, my Facebook page, or any of your favorite vendors.

I do hang out a little on social media, though I'm more of a lurker than a regular poster. Still, you can catch me there, mostly Instagram as of this writing. And I adore hearing from readers directly, so always feel free to email me!

Thanks again for reading THE SCAVENGER JOB!

~Kat

Don't miss the new season of the
Dragon Thief!

Starting with
THE CROWN OF KINGSHIP JOB

Keep reading for an excerpt!

THE CROWN OF KINGSHIP JOB

SEASON TWO OF THE DRAGON THIEF

EXCERPT

ONE

Myra was braced against the side of the glass-covered high rise, just after two in the morning, in downtown Manhattan two blocks from Wall St. when he found her. And not for nothing, but the fact that she was hanging by a rope, securely attached to a jump harness, and he wasn't, and didn't even need one because of the wings, was something that would probably always both amuse and annoy her.

"I'm in the middle of something," she said, as a cold spring breeze cooled her cheeks. It was a little embarrassing how easy it was for Christopher to find her. And while she was on a job, no less. She shouldn't be surprised. He'd been able to find her, even when she was on a job, since they'd met. But it was still embarrassing.

His massive wings beat the air gently, keeping him level with her. His expression was just shy of a smirk, which was good because she wasn't opposed to removing any smirks from his face by hitting him where it hurt.

The son of a dragon shifter king, Christopher —not Chris or he got grumpy—had one huge soft spot. Damsels in distress. Couldn't resist them. He considered it a real flaw in his character. Myra did not. In fact, it was one of the things she adored about him. But she was shameless about using his soft spot against him when she was embarrassed.

Which she was now.

She was an excellent thief and it dinged her pride that he was always able to sniff her out so easily. She must be losing some of her edge. Or maybe she'd allowed Christopher too close. Either way, it was a real pain in the ass that he could find her, no matter what, even when she'd gone out of her way to be unfindable.

"I have a job for you," Christopher said. "One you're going to want to take."

"I'm on a job," she pointed out, gesturing at the building and the tinted glass window she was currently braced against, her glass cutting tool halfway through the circular cut that would get her inside.

"They removed the bonds this morning," he said. "They aren't in there anymore."

She narrowed her eyes, glanced at the half-cut circle, then back at him as his wing beat swayed him a little closer to her. "How do you know that when I don't?"

And how had he known about the job she'd given herself?

Since they'd gotten more *involved*, she'd started to realize that just doing her own thing was a lot harder now than it had been a few months ago. There was someone there now, someone who cared where she was and what she was doing and if she died. And while that was nice on the one hand, it was also a little stifling on the other for someone who'd been on her own for a very long time now.

He wasn't trying to stifle her, she knew he wasn't. But she'd started to feel a little...locked in. Like she had to report her whereabouts to him, and run her jobs by him. That was her own issue. He really wasn't the one holding her back. But she'd started to plan jobs she didn't discuss with him, just to prove to herself that she was still a free agent. Their relationship hadn't, in fact, locked her up.

The problem was he could still find her, and he still somehow always knew what she was doing.

She wondered if he even realized that was starting to bother her.

"Do you want the job or not?" he asked, his tone a bit clipped.

Maybe he did know she was bothered. "Is it for your father?"

The last few times she'd worked for the dragon king, she'd gotten…well, not burned exactly. Because in the world of dragon shifters, getting "burned" meant something more than just not getting paid what she was owed. And actually, the dragon king had paid her what he owed her on those jobs. She'd just nearly gotten her killed. More than once. And worse even than nearly getting killed, the dragon king—and too many others—had starting to think of her as "his" thief. She was no one's thief. Not even Christopher's.

So she'd made it crystal clear, to everyone, that she had no intention of working for the dragon king ever again. Christopher had been onboard with that decision. His father was less gracious about it but had, outwardly, agreed.

"Something else," Christopher assured, his tone softening, his luminous blue-eyed gaze darting away from her before he looked at her again.

She tilted her head, gave him a narrow-eyed look. "Damsel in distress?"

He glanced away again, but even in the dark, with only the ambient city light to illuminate his face, she could clearly see the color staining his otherwise pale cheeks. Myra didn't try to hide her smug smile.

Christopher wasn't what someone might technically call handsome, but he was striking. Huge—and if his soft spot was damsels in distress, hers was tall men—and lean, with a lot of interesting angles in his broad features. Perpetually messy dark hair. Blue eyes. That still unexplained scar on his jaw under his beard scruff. The little scar on his forehead. Currently dressed in what she thought of as his flight uniform— barefoot, jeans, and no shirt so he could do the partial shift that gave him wings while he maintained most of the rest of his human form.

She liked the word compelling for him. That was the best way to describe him. Compelling. But the fact that he fit so precisely into a category she was weak for, unfortunately, tipped the balance between them more often than she'd like to admit. And very much complicated her already complicated feelings for him.

"There's money involved," he said.

She shrugged, dangling from her rope now instead of bracing against the building. She hid her grin when a muscle in his jaw flexed as he took in her even more precarious position. "You know it's not the money for me."

It had been, once up on a time. But that got old fast. Now, she used all her magical thieving skills for jobs she found interesting. Stealing things that should have been impossible to steal. And if the mark was someone who didn't deserve to have something stolen from them, she returned the item. If they were someone who deserved to have something stolen from them, or wouldn't even notice the theft... Well, she had alternative paths she took for those items.

Her favorite game now, though, was sticking it to the powerful and wealthy. That was where the real fun happened. Which was why she was dangling outside a skyscraper looking to steal bonds from a wealthy investment company that had some dodgy practices, including investing in some very hinky businesses.

"There's a rich asshole who will suffer if we win," Christopher said. Because he understood her various weaknesses as much as she understood his.

And damn him, that was the one that got her.

She glanced at her half-cut circle. "No bonds inside?"

"No bonds," he confirmed, crossing his arms over his massive chest, all his muscles flexing as he pumped his wings in gentle downbeats to keep level with her. The shimmer of the purple and yellow scales over his chest blended into his wings, the light reflecting off the scales winking at her.

She pursed her lips and nodded. Then removed her glass cutting tool, folded it back up, put it into its zip pocket on her fitted black vest, and detached from her rope, dropping into free fall toward the Manhattan street.

He caught her when she was only half way down the fifty-seven-story skyscraper, scooping her out of the air with a scowl and beating his wings hard a few times to get them back up over the top of the skyline, the glittery lights of the city falling away beneath them.

She wrapped her arms around his neck and grinned at the side of his face. "So... Tell me about this job."

Season Two of the Dragon Thief begins with

THE CROWN OF KINGSHIP JOB

Out Now!!

Join Kat's Newsletter

Stay Up-to-Date

On all Kat's News, Updates, and fun extras

New Subscriber Get Two Exclusive Stories Just for Signing up!

bit.ly/KatSimonsNewsletter

Paranormal Romance

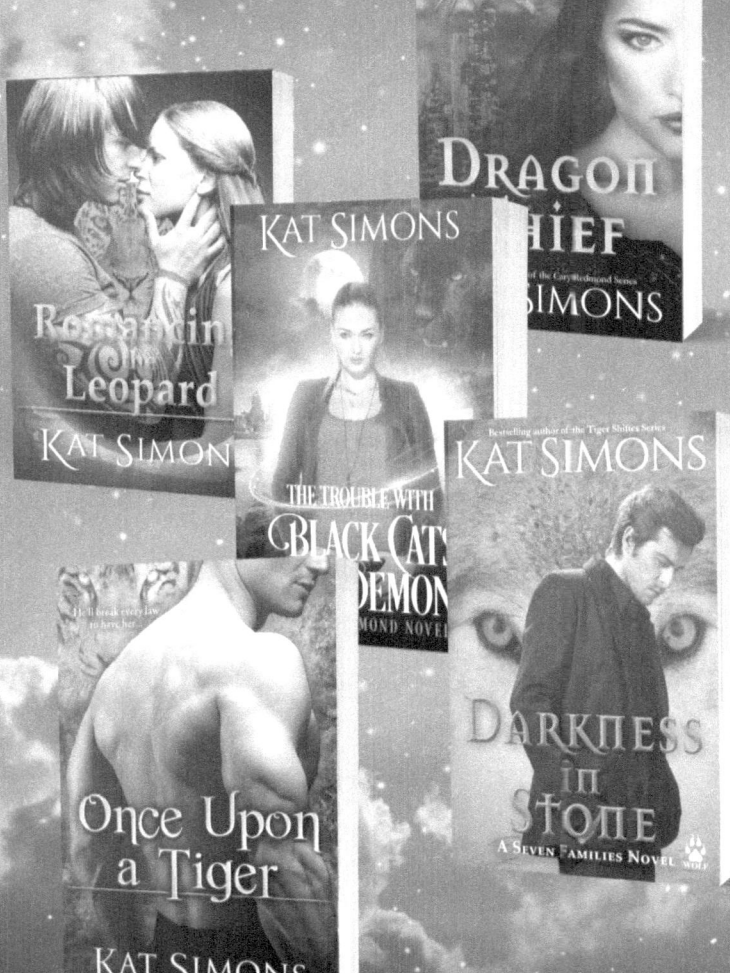

THE DRAGON THIEF SERIES

DRAGON THIEF
SIMONS

KAT SIMONS

Romancing the Leopard

KAT SIMONS

THE TROUBLE WITH BLACK CATS DEMONS
DEMOND NOVEL

He'll break every law to have her...

Once Upon a Tiger

KAT SIMONS

Bestselling author of the Tiger Shifter Series

KAT SIMONS

DARKNESS IN STONE
A SEVEN FAMILIES NOVEL
WOLF

From
KAT SIMONS

Thanks for Reading!

To celebrate the end of Season One of the Dragon Thief series, here's a special discount code just for readers to KatSimonsBooks

LOVEMC10

Enter this code at checkout for a 10% discount off everything in your cart!

Thank you for reading!

KATSIMONSBOOKS.COM

KATSIMONSBOOKS

Mystery

Urban Fantasy

Romance

And More!

Books By Kat Simons

Dragon Thief Series

Season One

Dragon Thief

The Chicago Job

The Poisons Book Job

The Vault Job

The Femme Fatale Job

The Scavenger Job

Season Two

The Crown of Kingship Job

The Green Scroll Job

The Payback Job

Pick Your Genre Collections

Who Steals a Dragon

The Cary Redmond Series

* The Trouble Black Cats and Demons * The Trouble
with Ghouls and Serial Killers * The Trouble with

Leopard Queens and Shifter Wars * The Trouble with Baby Gods and Vampires * The Trouble with Magic and Faery Curses * The Trouble with Wizards and Old Enemies * The Trouble with Death and Demon Gods

The Cary Redmond Series Box Set Books 1-3

Cary Redmond Short Stories

* When Cary Met Jaxer * When Cary Met Pickles * When Cary Met Marianne * When Cary Met Lucy * When Cary Met Angie * Cary and Deacon (Try to) Go on a Date * Date Night Take Two * Third Date's the Charm * Cary vs the Goblin King * Dinner with the Joneses * Cary and the Cursed Jack-O'-Lantern * Cary and the Demon Witch * Cary Goes to Hawaii * Cary Holidays * Cary and Dragons and Goblins * Cary's Galentine's Day * Cary at the Haunt and Howl * Cary's Leprechaun Troubles * Cary's Beltane Night Out *

When Cary Met the Good Guys (Collection 1)

Dates, Dinners, and Other Disasters (Collection 2)

Witches and Weavers and Ghosts, Oh Boy (Collection 3)

A Very Cary Holiday (Collection 4)

Romancing the Leopard: A Tiger Shifters-Cary Redmond Crossover Novel

Tiger Shifters Series

* Once Upon a Tiger * Along Came a Tiger * Here There Be Tigers * Her Tiger To Take * To Tempt a Tiger * Down Will Come Tiger * To Catch a Tiger * What a Tiger Wants * Taming Her Tiger

Tiger Shifters Series Vol 1 (Books 1 - 3)

Tiger Shifters Series Vol 2 (Books 4 - 6)

Seven Families Series

Wolf Family

Darkness in Stone

Redemption in Stone

Fated in Stone

Wolf in Stone: A Seven Families Box Set, Books 1-3

Demon Witch Series

Howling Dreadful

Moonlit Strange

Bone Lantern Witch

Spiderweb Witch

Storm Shadow Witch

Darkling Mist Witch

Joan of Kerry Series

Joan of Kerry: Joan and the Abhartach

Joan and the Leprechaun

Joan and the Kraken

Joan and the Selkie

Joan and the Goblins

Haunts and Howls Collections

Haunts and Howls and Guardian Spells

Haunts and Howls Where Demons Dwell

Haunts and Howls and Jesters Bells

Haunts and Howls and Fairy Dales

*Tombstone Wizard * The Unshattered Sword * Destiny Through the Cats Eyes * Going Out of Business: Everything's for Sale * Anger Management * Demonic Dates * Friday's Curious Shop * The Museum of Small Art's Everyman * Burning Inside a Stone Circle * Bored Questless * I Just Ate a Bug * Ting Ling * Sophie Saves the World * Black Water Hawthorns *To Dance in Fallow Fields at Midnight *

More Books by Kat Simons

Contemporary Romances

Designed for You

Poinsettias and Possibilities

Mystery and Thrillers

Ross and O'Neill Adventures

Galileo's Pendulum

Percy James Mysteries

Movies May Murder

Cookies Can't Crime

Diamonds Do Damage

Replicas Risk Ruin

Vacation Deadly: An Action Adventure Thriller
Collection

About the Author

Kat Simons earned her Ph.D. in animal behavior, working with animals as diverse as dolphins and deer. She brought her experience and knowledge of biology to her paranormal romance and urban fantasy fiction, where she delights in taking nature and turning it on its ear. She writes urban fantasy, contemporary fantasy, and paranormal romance in series which combine action adventure, the otherworldly, and a frequent dose of sexy romance.

The newest book in her bestselling romantic urban fantasy series about Protector Cary Redmond, The Trouble with Shifters and Fae Courts, sees a new direction for the intrepid Protector, her sexy leopard shifter mate, and the entire crew. Kat also launched a new novella length Paranormal Romance series that follows the adventures of a magical thief and the dragon shifter prince she just can't seem to shake—and really doesn't want to. The first season of the Dragon Thief series released throughout 2024.

Season Two begins in 2025 with The Crown of Kingship Job.

For something a little different, Kat also publishes fantasy, science fiction, and the occasional hockey romance under the name Isabo Kelly (https://www.isabokelly.com).

After traveling the world, living in places like Hawaii, Germany, and Ireland, Kat now lives in New York City with her family and a library's worth of books.

For more on Kat and her future books

Website: https://www.katsimons.com/
Newsletter: https://bit.ly/KatSimonsNewsletter

KatSimonsBooks
https://www.katsimonsbooks.com
https://www.TheCafeatKatSimonsBooks.com

Social Media
Facebook Page: https://www.facebook.com/
KatSimonsAuthor
BookBub: https://www.bookbub.com/authors/kat-
simons
Bluesky: https://bsky.app/profile/katsimons.bsky.
social
Instagram: https://www.instagram.com/isabokelly/
Threads: https://www.threads.net/@isabokelly